About

Ajay K Pandey grew up in the modest NTPC township of Rihand Nagar with big dreams. He studied Engineering in Electronics at IERT (Allahabad) and MBA at IIMM (Pune) before taking up a job in a corporate firm. He is currently working with Cognizant, Pune. He grew up with a dream of becoming a teacher, but destiny landed him in the IT field. Travelling, trekking and reading novels are his hobbies.

Travelling to different places has taught him about different cultures and people, and makes him wonder how despite all the differences, there is a bond that unites them. Trekking always inspires him to deal with challenges like a sport. Reading is perhaps what makes him feel alive.

You are the Best Wife is his debut book based on his life events and lessons. Apart from writing, he wants to follow his role model Mother Teresa, and make some contribution to the society. He aspires to start a charitable trust that would support aged people and educate special children.

After his debut book *You Are the Best Wife*, Ajay has authored bestselling titles *Her Last Wish* and *You are the Best Friend*.

: *AuthorAjayPandey*   : *@AjayPandey_08*
: *@author_ajaykpandey* :   : *ajaypandey0807@gmail.com*

By the same author:

You Are the Best Wife

Her Last Wish

"... a bestselling book is made"

—*Scroll.in*

"The real love story will pull you in a pool of emotions."

—*Jagran*

"There are some books that are not just stories but reflection of realities of life. *You are the Best Wife* is one such book.

—*Writers Melon*

"The Indian author has given reasons to believe that India has not only given good tech-heads, but are delivering literary moths too."

—*The Truth India*

"... sold over a lakh copies ... connected with the masses in a way no previous author has ever done."

—*Book Geeks.in*

"The loving heart of a beautiful soul Bhavna, encouraged Ajay to fight back and start looking at life in a positive way."

—*India Café 24*

"It is one of the purest, heart-warming love stories I ever read..."

—*Salisonline.in*

A *Girl*
to Remember

AJAY K PANDEY

Srishti
PUBLISHERS & DISTRIBUTORS

Srishti Publishers & Distributors
A unit of AJR Publishing LLP
212A, Peacock Lane
Shahpur Jat, New Delhi – 110 049
editorial@srishtipublishers.com

First published by
Srishti Publishers & Distributors in 2018

Printed and bound in India

The book is dedicated to Ankita.
I know there is no need for formalities, but still…
Because of you, I feel lucky and blessed.

Acknowledgements

Hi friends,

I wish to start by telling you that writing this book has been a tough deal for me. Not just because I have left my comfort zone and tried something new, but also because this story is distinctive in many ways. It's based on a true declaration of a friend who doesn't want to highlight his identity. I have heard his story and made many changes, but not altered the basic message – confession is the best punishment.

A few of my readers have complained about the tragic endings of my stories. But friends, sometimes, the journey is more important than the destination. I hope you understand this deep felt message and continue loving me the way you have.

My gratitude to my entire family, who stood by me and decided to take each step with me.

Thanks to my author friend, Priyanka Lal, for getting rid of the unwanted words and making this book a smooth read. She is someone who knows how to change a regular girl into a dream girl.

Acknowledgements

Thank you, Jayanta Kumar Bose and Arup Bose, for showing your faith in me.

My editor friend Stuti, for helping me make this book a charming and desirable read. This book would not have been possible without you.

Heartfelt gratitude and special thanks to Jayanthi Ramesh, Satish Sundaram and Deepthi Talwar.

Many thanks to my friends from the film world – Adit Singh (Producer at Seven Horse Production) and Ajay Mohan Kaul (Director and Editor).

A big thank you to my readers for accepting my crazy stories. I try hard to reply to each and every message and comment that I get. Believe it or not, it is you who have made me what I am today. I take this opportunity to thank all the wonderful hearts who stood in my support in their own individual way. Your reviews and feedback are the silent but efficient way to promote an author. I would like to thank the following reader friends who have now become a part of my life, more like my extended family –Subhajit Das, Sheetal Poojari, Anandhini Iyappan, Lalita Sharma, Lata Sharma, Mona Sharma, Pavan Sharma, Grishma Ninave, Aparna Jayaram, Ankita Kumar, Lavanya Rajanala, Heena Patel, Tejal Dave, Sunaina Kapoor, Sweety Chhatwal Johar, Shruti Kamla, Neha Yadav, Manjusha Gurajada, Abantika Chattopadhyay, Tania Chatterjee, Guru Priya, Merlin Felisha, and Arpita Saxena.

Acknowledgements

A big hug to you all. Thank you for making me an author, though I would always politely ask you to treat me as your author friend.

Never surrender!

Ajay

Acknowledgements

A woman is a mother, a sister, a friend or a daughter to someone. You can understand these relationships better when you become a father or a husband. A relationship is the mother of all feelings. You will realise... she is not just a body; she is much more than that.'

— Mom

Prologue

2015
Pune

The famous psychoanalyst Carl Jung once said that everything has two sides. I couldn't agree more. I also firmly believe that every living being has two sides to their personality. One is usually good, and the other bad. One half is positive, and the other, negative. One side is where the angels rule, the other is where they fear to tread. This story is about the demon that lives within us, skilfully silencing the angel and winning over with its dark temptations.

I am Neel Kumar, comfortably serving as a mathematics teacher in the posh urban DAV Private School. The food and accommodation is taken care of, the pay is enough to meet my needs and desires, and life is good in general. But I am a slave of my body. I tried to hide my desire, but the demon inside me came out to quench itself when it saw naked legs. A bare, hairless, soft, long leg triggers the monster in me. I guess, there is something wrong with my mind.

This is my story, and how hard it really was for me to hear the voice of my heart, thanks to the girl – no, a girl to remember.

One

2015
DAV Private School, Aundh, Pune

The posh co-education school was one of the best in the city, centrally located and sophisticated. Most students came from affluent and well-to-do families, and the school provided them with ample facilities and modern amenities, obviously for a comparable fee. Looking at the way parents left their kids at school in a hurry made me feel that they came to dump their kids there, to have peace and freedom for six hours.

The staff accommodation was within the premises, about one kilometre away from the school building. It was a convenient arrangement for bachelors like me, who had to spend a lot of time and effort to find a decent place.

But the previous night, I had been asked to leave the staff colony. Though the recent rumours doing the rounds in school had prepared me for it, somewhat. In trying to find the reason behind the order, I was told the *official* reason – the revision in rules allowed the staff quarters to be given out to families only. Bachelors were not allowed. But a whole lot of my bachelor colleagues were still there, cosy and comfortable.

The *actual* reason that they did not and could not disclose, however, was – they assumed I had slept with a student in my flat the previous afternoon on the pretext of teaching her. The girl was a student of mine, a minor, and the only daughter of an influential father – perfect recipe to ruin my life and career.

Honestly, I was not a saint. In fact, I saw myself more as a demon, if anything. But this time, I wasn't at fault. Events had just unravelled in a way that made me look like the culprit. I have indulged in a lot of relationships, mostly no strings attached, but never with my students. I have never forced myself on any girl. Nor have I ever passed a wrong comment out loud. I might be imagining them naked in my mind and saying and doing what my senses found bliss in, but I have never crossed the barrier of being human. There were fragments of humanity in me.

I was now looking for an accommodation and wondering how I'd go about finding another job for myself if the school decided to throw me out for good. As I sat impatiently in a property dealer's office just across the school gate, I had more things running on my mind than the chaotic traffic on the road outside. With three big bags on my side, taking up most of the dealer's office space, anyone could guess that I was relocating in a hurry.

I sat in front of the broker, quite hopeful. He looked at me with an expression which smelled of irritation. I noticed his office was well-furnished and luxurious, and my request for a cheap paying guest accommodation option must have put him off a bit. Finding an accommodation in Pune is quite a task for a bachelor, I told you. Pune is known as the 'Oxford of the East', thanks to quite a few popular educational institutions in the city. Nearly half of the total international students in the country study in Pune, so you can imagine the rush. Add to it that it's an IT hub, so the city also has a good number of well-earning people from other states. The rent business is good and flourishing, and brokers earned handsomely.

I knew it was going to be tough, given this man's attitude, but what other option did I have! As my eyes travelled to his face, they stopped momentarily at his oily neck, where a thick gold chain hung. It instantly reminded me of the steel chain I often used for securing my luggage while travelling in trains.

His dark brown face had turned darker and gloomier when he realised I was not one of the rich customers. After his yellow eyes had finished looking at me with disdain, his thick black lips finally moved to say, 'Mr Neel, it's very difficult to get a flat at such short notice. Plus, your price range is too low.' His single sentence, spoken in a heavy Marathi accent, had drained me of a fistful of hope.

'I am comfortable with a PG as well,' I said in a mortified tone, consoling myself more than the broker.

He took in a long breath of exasperation, picked up his expensive phone, and began browsing. 'Let me try to find a PG for you...'

'Any luck?' I asked hesitantly after about twenty minutes of seeing him fidget with his phone.

He gave me a look which said, I was the source of all his troubles right now.

I had been in his office for almost an hour now. I was desperate to find a place before school got over for the day, lest students, saw me and started asking questions to which I had no answers. But my destiny had been written with ash, it seemed.

Soon enough, students started coming out of the school, towards their guardians. Most had the air-conditioned school buses waiting to take them home, a few had fancy, chauffer driven cars picking them up, some waited for autos, and a few others for their shared rides. One could hear a cacophony of screaming and giggling kids, cautioning parents, gossiping moms and maids, and the super active hawkers selling ice-creams, colas and candies.

4

I looked at all this from the transparent glass window of the broker's office. My eyes fell on a hawker selling masala cola. It was a hot February day, and just one look at the poster of the chilled cola glass on his cart had me salivating. I had not had anything to eat or drink since morning in the rush to vacate. My dehydrated self was demanding a cool refreshing cola.

I looked at the broker with his eyes digging in to his phone and absently said, 'Sir, I will go out for a drink.'

He did not even nod in response. Quite sure he had heard me, I dragged myself towards the door.

'O Master saab… Teacher sir… take your luggage with you. There is no guarantee here.'

'But I will be back in a couple of minutes,' I said, quite surprised.

He looked at me exasperatedly. It was the longest eye contact we had in the whole time I was there. His pot belly was moving back and forth with every breath, his shirt buttons on the belly threatening to fly off at any time. This man seemed like the one responsible for malnutrition in India.

'Please carry your things with you,' he said with a grave expression and got back to his phone.

It was a polite way to shoo me away. I took my luggage and dragged myself to the cola serving man, requesting for a glass. The cola man made such a performance out of mixing ice, lemon and that patented masala – that's still a mystery for most of us – before offering me the drink.

I took a sip. I couldn't taste the cola, but the entire blend was cooling down my anxiety a bit, and tasted nice.

I had my back towards the school gate because of obvious reasons, but instinctively turned around to see if there were any familiar faces. That's when I noticed a pair of unblinking eyes looking towards me. It stood out so peculiarly because it was an unknown girl.

She started walking towards the same stall, perhaps for a glass of cola. She was wearing the school uniform. The short skirt ended just above her knees, and her striped shirt was tucked in neatly. She looked like a regular girl, nothing remarkable in her appearance. As she purposefully strode towards us, I realized, she was coming towards me, and not the hawker. Her eyes were set on me, still unblinking, and that was a tad bit disturbing. I think the fear of the word having spread in school about my suspension was gnawing my insides, and that made me quite conscious of this mundane event. I felt suspicious of her, because the way she looked at me, made me feel she knew me and my

5

secret. In a matter of a few seconds, she was standing right in front of me, a spark of recognition in her eyes.

She was thin, tall and fair to the point of being white. Out of her otherwise reed thin body, her abdomen seemed to swell in a strange way, making her look strangely stocky from the middle. Her legs peeking from under the skirt had no curvy appeal. They seemed more like a pair of bamboo sticks supporting a thin frame.

'Good afternoon, Neel sir,' came her sweet and timid voice. 'Why are you carrying so many bags? Are you going somewhere?' the young girl asked. Her voice and face showed genuine concern.

Despite the circumstances, I was pleasantly surprised. I wondered why she would enquire after a teacher who barely knew her.

'Actually, I am shifting to a new place,' I answered her with an attempted straight face. Her brown eyes were almost like mine and something in her demeanour made me feel I knew her very well. What made her so familiar, I wondered?

'Sir, I am Pihu. Class tenth student.' Her voice was quite sweet, which is common at her age. It is only as we grow up that the voice and the world around us starts getting less pleasant and polite.

'If you don't mind me asking, sir,' she began humbly, '... have you left the staff accommodation already? And where are you shifting to? I hope you are not leaving the school...' her voice trailed off. The sudden dip in the voice showed she was somehow hurt by the idea.

How I wished a property dealer to have asked the question about the accommodation.

'Oh yes, I have surrendered the school flat. The food at the mess wasn't very good.'

'Hmm. So, you've already found another accommodation?' she asked again.

This girl – who had appeared sweet, humble and concerned till now – was now beginning to look too intrusive. I did not wish to give her explanations or anymore lies. I had enough going on already, and too many questions could disclose what had brought me here. I could avoid more rumours about me, least of all through these seemingly harmless students.

'Yes,' I said and turned around to return the glass to the hawker.

Something in my sleep-deprived, pale face must have given away the fact that the "yes" was a fake. I could hear the hollowness in my voice while saying it, and prayed that this little girl had missed noticing it.

'If you want, I can help you,' she offered politely, without insisting this time, giving me a few seconds to weigh my options.

'Help me about what?' I asked innocently. But deep inside, my heart was running a marathon, wishing with every beat to hear something positive.

'We have a place available for rent in our house,' she said and my eyes snapped up at hers in a moment. She added as an afterthought, 'Our tenant recently moved abroad.'

Feeling exhilarated that I at least had an option now, I wanted to hug Pihu and cry out of happiness. I have heard of miracles happening, but they had never happened with me. After sitting hopeless for almost half the day, this blessing walking up to me was nothing less than a miracle. Luck never favoured me – neither as a child, nor now. But this girl had given me a new hope. All that said, I could not express my enthusiasm and happiness. Not only could it land me in trouble again, but it was definitely a wrong strategy to express happiness in front of a landlord, or landlord's daughter in this case.

'What would be the rent?' I asked hesitatingly, as I knew most kids in this school came from posh areas.

'Whatever you would like to pay, sir,' she said. I wondered if it was sarcasm, but soon I was sure she was being respectful.

I glanced at the cola serving man, wondering if the drink was spiked! Was I hallucinating? The man smiled at me, showing off his yellow-brown teeth. The sheer glimpse of those teeth assured me I was not dreaming. I was being offered a house on rent by a girl, who was apparently my student, and the rent was for me to decide!

'Please confirm with your parents, Pihu. I have already found a flat. If I take up your offer, let go of that flat and your family refuses... I don't want any such hassles later,' I said, trying to keep my voice calm.

'Yeah, your point is valid, sir. Let me speak to my mom,' she said, pulling her cell phone out. Taking a few steps away from me, she made the call that was to decide my fate. I wasn't sure how things would eventually turn out, but the way it had gone till now, I had high hopes. My heart sank for a bit when I saw the timid Pihu speak aggressively into the phone. She was walking restlessly as she spoke to her mother.

I crossed my fingers as I looked at the unusual girl. I could gather that she was arguing with her mom – for me. I was quite surprised, but did not take a second more to offer a few bribes to god. 'Please, help me this time, god. I swear I will not stare at anyone's legs for the rest of my life.'

She looked at me from the corner of her eyes, disconnected the call, and started walking towards me again. The voting was done. The decision had been made, and I was waiting with bated breath, like a Big Boss finalist, whose result was to be announced.

'So, what is the decision?' I asked, failing to keep away the excitement from my voice miserably.

She asked instead, 'Sir, you have only these three bags?' Her triumphant smile was somewhat reassuring.

'Yes!' I managed to say after I breathed out the air I had been holding in my lungs.

'Let's get going, then!' she said with a smile touching her ears, and I couldn't thank my stars enough for this happy coincidence. We quickly hailed an auto and she instructed him about the place we were headed to; my new home, if all went well – Panchsheel Nagar.

The ride was quiet, except for Pihu giving the driver directions to her house. I sat back and looked out, feeling overwhelmed with the way things had turned out in the last twenty-four hours or so. From the settled life I was enjoying, I was back to where I had been a few years ago – homeless and penniless. Now, as the auto neared the destination, doubts began to flood my head.

I wondered what I was going to say to Pihu's parents, because I did not know anything about her. She hadn't existed for me till a few moments back, and now I had all my hopes pinned on her.

'So, which class are you in, Pihu?'

9

'Tenth, sir.'

'Oh! I taught math to the entire ninth standard batch last year, but I don't recognize you,' I said honestly, trying to read her face. I had seen her somewhere, no doubt, but why I wasn't able to place her was beyond me!

'That's because last year I was in tenth only. I failed,' she said as if in a whisper, eyes downcast, and visibly upset.

Of course! That's how I knew her. It was a big deal in school as she was the only one who failed in tenth. Without batting an eyelid, my mind categorized her into a spoilt brat. We have a tendency of judging a student by his or her marks, and I was no different.

I asked her a few more questions about her class teacher, subjects of interest and extra-curricular activities, just to know a bit more about her, in general. I asked about her preparations for this year's exams, and she gave a squeak for an answer. Not that I was much concerned about her preparation or result; I just wanted to make sure I was able to convince her parents completely, by hook or crook. Even if I had to falsely praise Pihu or make up a story.

Just then, the auto hit a speed breaker. Perhaps the driver had not seen it coming, and the jolt sent us flying in our seats. When we landed back, she had shifted slightly closer to me and her skirt had gone up a bit, giving me a small view of her thighs. As much as I tried to think of other things, testosterone hit my system. It was like a million unwanted organisms getting activated inside me, ushering me to a high. I could never understand why this particular body part in women fascinated me. I turned my gaze away to the roads. Pihu was my student, and perhaps landlord, too – in a way. I didn't want any trouble after what had happened at school recently.

When I looked back at her to see if she had noticed this change in my demeanour, I saw some sort of excitement on her face, which I found discomforting.

'Sir, you know, you are my favourite teacher!' She was beaming at me.

I could have handled it easily if she had said those words simply, like many other students did. But she had taken my hand in hers and almost rested her head on my shoulder while saying it. Like I was her boyfriend. I wondered what she was up to. Was she planning to take a nap on my shoulder?! This gesture inevitably fuelled the thoughts already brewing in my head. I took my eyes away from her and looked at the sky instead. Not again, god!

I had just promised him that I won't stare at women, and here, the supreme deity was testing my capacity. If I could really stick by my words and control my nasty desires.

I focused my energy on her words instead, and smiled fictitiously before replying, 'That's really nice to hear. I am overwhelmed. Thanks.'

I wanted to hold her shoulders, shake her into reality and ask her to shift away from me. But that would have been too risky a proposition, given that I still needed her help. Keeping the conversation casual, I continued, 'Did you speak to your parents about the rent? I mean, I know you spoke to your mom... Is she okay with whatever I wish to pay?'

She nodded a yes. My breath caught up in excitement.

'What about your father? Don't you need to check with him too?'

She looked mighty displeased with this question. Her smile vanished and she turned sad. Unknowingly, I had embarked upon a prohibited subject.

She tried to appear unaffected when she replied, 'I don't have a father.'

Two

When Pihu asked the auto driver to finally stop, we had travelled about four kilometres from school. I got down and pulled out the bags. Looking around, I was nothing less than astonished. We were in the posh Baner area, and in every house's driveway stood a BMW or a Mercedes. You would think they were buying cars to shoo each other away; each one was better and grander than the previous. The potted plants and the hedges over boundary walls grew perfectly, neatly maintained and quite charming. As far as my eyes could see, I could not spot a single thing out of place. No stray animals, no litter, not even overgrown bushes - it was amazing. There were shady trees on both sides of the lane, and some bore flowers also. It seemed like a dream sequence, till I heard a bark.

A few dogs of breeds I did not even know the names of approached the metal gates of their respective houses on hearing a strange vehicle break the quiet of their lazy afternoon.

Pihu turned around and approached a house that seemed the smallest in the locality. It was then that I noticed the two-storied house which had been behind my back till now. The house was screaming, "I am very old." The faded walls confirmed that it had been a long time since someone had paid any heed to it. Compared to the neighbouring houses, this house seemed from another world. It needed emergency treatment for an upliftment, given the overgrown shrubs in the garden, the peeling paint and a sad outer facade.

A great location and poor maintenance says a lot about the financial status of the owner. Now I could understand why this strange girl was so desperate to offer me an accommodation on rent. Maybe the owners needed an emergency facelift too.

'Sir, the ground floor is available for rent. Please wait here. I will get the keys for you.' Pihu chirped, eager to show me around. There was a strange enthusiasm in her, which made me somewhat uncomfortable. Not something out of place, though, as I have seen similar emotions and its expression in kids when they see their favourite relative, or when someone offers them their favourite ice cream. I told myself I would have to get accustomed to her over excitement around me all the time, rather than feel taken aback by it.

As Pihu had climbed up the stairs to get the key, I had looked around at the unkempt garden and the small parking space that definitely could not accommodate a fancy car. The house was a definite misfit in a posh locality. But at the end of it all, if this girl actually lived here, and I would get accommodation in this locality after being thrown out of the hostel. I would have to admit – miracles do happen.

I looked around again and saw Pihu climbing up the stairs at leisure. It seemed like a task for her. *The lazy girl.*

Pihu finally came back, after a long long time, with a bunch of keys with her. She opened the chipped wooden door on the ground floor.

She pushed open the door and entered swiftly, moving around the room to switch on the lights and fan. I was curious to see what this place looked like, but was hesitant to go inside. An empty house and a teenage girl were not really a recommended combination for me. I did not wish to give anyone a wrong impression. Too much had gone wrong in a matter of a day. My career, character and almost my entire life was at stake here.

'Come in, sir,' Pihu bent her head to peep out at me.

I stepped in. The house seemed spacious. The sitting room was flanked by two rooms. Behind the room on the right was a smaller room, which was the kitchen. In the centre of the kitchen was an old but sturdy wooden table, with two chairs. Below the cooking slab were wooden racks to store things. In one corner was a small sink for washing dishes. Next to the kitchen was a narrow but clean bathroom.

The bedroom had a double bed, along with mattresses and a couple of soft looking pillows, which lacked covers for now. There was a wooden wardrobe lining one wall of the room, a full-length mirror in the centre. Crossing the room to have a look, I happened to glance at my reflection. The only word that came to mind on seeing the man in the mirror was exhausted.

I raised my head to thank the lord. I had a roof over my head. That was when I saw the ceiling fan, quite sleek and comparatively new. After the facilities at the staff flat, this place seemed like a hotel with essential amenities. I was extremely happy to have landed at this place. And then the worrying thought stuck me - the rent.

We walked around and saw the place, eventually returning to the sitting room, where I had left my bags. I didn't see any

15

film of dust which is usual in locked-up houses. The place had not been vacant for too long.

Pihu made herself comfortable on a woven chair placed around a round wooden table, and gestured at me to take the other chair. She told me with a wide smile that we were waiting for her mother.

I was trying hard to organise the chaotic thoughts running all over my mind when I heard someone call out.

'Piiihuuuu....'

The feminine, soft voice was loving, yet firm to flaunt her connection with Pihu.

'Mom! I am here,' Pihu replied in a similar loving tone.

A moment later, a woman in loose fitting dark blue jeans and a flowy yellow top walked into the sitting room. I looked at Pihu, then at the woman, to notice the uncanny similarity in their features, confirming to me that she was the "mom".

Pihu looked much like her mother, but something was amiss. Perhaps a lively spark. I don't know. And this woman, she did not look like a mother to a seventeen-year-old at all. There was no superfluous fat anywhere, the long nose on her oval face was sharp, her high cheekbones gave her face a strange charm, her skin glowed, and she was wearing a light pink gloss on her thin lips. Her hair was cut short, and the boyish cut delicately framed her face. I also took in her delicate neck, and the way her top hugged her breasts, flowing over her flat belly. My eyes had lingered where I could see the jeans meeting the top. The devil within me had wanted to touch, explore some more. I was almost wishing for the fan to work its magic and sweep the top up a bit. As Pihu went forth and hugged her gorgeous mother, my eyes waited at her shapely behind, then travelled down the length of the leg, concealed from my sight. There was a lot running in my mind, but the words that rang the loudest in my head were, "She is the landlord!"

When there is a good flat in front of you and not much money in the pocket, then the landlord deserves more respect than any other Lord.

'Hi, how are you, sir?' the melodious voice asked me as she turned around to look at me.

I put forth my best puppy face and gave her a polite smile in return. I did not have a tail, or else I would have started wagging it, to grandly welcome the owner of the house.

'I am good, ma'am. How about you?'

She had addressed me as sir. I knew she was older to me, but this word is a nomenclature for me by virtue of my profession. In the education industry, once you become a teacher, the entire universe – students' parents, their grandparents, their children in future, and everyone who as much as gets to know your profession – addresses you as sir.

'Great!' She extended her hand to take mine into hers softly. 'I am Annu.'

I really liked her uninhibited handshake. 'I am Neel Kumar.'

She gave me a queer look, as if she was trying to decipher me. I knew what checking out is, and I also know when someone stares at you suspiciously. Her look was somewhere between the two. I thought she had discovered something unusual on my face. Or maybe someone she knew looked like me. Perhaps it was a family hobby to stare at a stranger's faces.

I noticed she had the same brown eyes as me and Pihu. It was an amazing coincidence.

'How is the place?' Annu smiled at me. 'Hope,you liked the room. I know it's a little untidy…' she mock-glared at her child, '…but she informed me at the eleventh hour!'

She was calling this place untidy! She had definitely never seen how bachelors lived.

'No issues… It's good enough.'

'Is this all of your luggage?' she looked at my bags.

'Yes!'

I really wanted to lie down and rest for a while. My body had been through a lot in the past twenty-four hours, and needed some rest. But it seemed I still needed to answer some questions. Any wrong answer could push me back into flat hunt.

'Are you shifting with your family, sir?'

My throat went dry. I wondered if I could lose this place if the answer did not match up with Annu's expectations. After the experience at the realtor's office, I did not think I had the courage to bear it.

The demon in me urged me to pass the buck on to Pihu. Why had she not explained my situation before offering the place to me? Now here I stood, forced to contemplate between lying and keeping the place.

But Pihu was just a teenager, my heart said. She had done enough by helping me the way she had. I summoned all my courage and said, 'I am not married, and my family lives in another city. So, I live alone.'

Annu's face turned grim. A smiling landlord turning serious. But I was surprised. My answer had brought a smile on Pihu's face. I was a little shaken to realise that my marital status had affected her and her mother so differently.

'Excuse me, sir,' Annu said politely and turned to her daughter. 'Pihu, can we talk for a moment?' She stepped out of the sitting room.

For the first time since we met, I felt bad for the young girl. Was she in trouble?

Pihu turned to look at me as she followed Annu out of the house. I tried to return a sympathetic look, but she winked at me, smiling slyly. I was shocked! Clearly. After all, it was not expected behaviour when you met someone for the first time. Especially your school teacher.

I turned to my dried-up phone. I stared at it, as if it was the greatest invention on earth.

Their private discussion was not exactly private. Naturally, in a quiet locality like theirs, you could hear even whispers. Annu seemed clearly uncomfortable with having a single man living in her house.

The mother-daughter duo argued for some time, both throwing glances in the direction of the house time and again – Annu, agitated; Pihu, overexcited. But finally, they seemed to reach a consensus.

'Sir, sorry, Pihu had not given me all your details,' she said hesitantly.

The word 'sorry' stuck to my ears and I was sure this was a polite way of asking me to get lost. I didn't know what to say, for my hopes were crashing.

I looked up only when I heard Annu say, 'It's okay…'

'What did you tell your mother, Pihu?' I asked with a fake bright smile, hoping it would lighten the mood a bit.

'Sir, I told her you are just like a family member,' Pihu said innocently, but I did not miss the strange spark in her eyes as she said that. Teenagers confused me, and Pihu was turning out to be the most challenging one to tackle.

I gave her a frustrated look. She was smiling for no reason. I wanted to explode on Pihu, give her a piece of my mind for having wasted my day. I would have pestered the broker into finding a place for me by now. But she seemed to be happily lost in a world of her own creation.

I cursed myself. Why had I believed this girl's words? I resigned to my fate and decided to make a move.

'I am sorry, ma'am. This is all a big miscommunication, I think,' I said, looking at Pihu who retained her strange smile, and then looking at Annu who looked flushed. 'I had no intention to put you in such a tight spot. But you don't have to worry too much. I will find another place. It's absolutely fine,' I lied seamlessly, faking a perfect smile. I had mastered the difficult art of lying. After all, I had practised it my entire life.

Annu suddenly flashed a genuine smile and said, 'It's okay, sir… no trouble at all. You can stay here.'

I looked up at her to gauge whether this was a joke. But no, she was smiling, and nodding her head. Annu's words made my day. The million-dollar, ear to ear smile on my oval face turned it into a perfectly circular penny.

'Just one request, sir. Since you will be living here on your own, we will close the second room at the back. I hope that's okay.' She had barely finished when I nodded my head, accepting her condition. She quickly added, 'Pihu and I stay on the first floor. You are free to use the terrace whenever you want.'

I nodded, relieved, happy and quite charged up.

Annu then led the way into the house and updated me about the house and amenities in detail, like a pro. She showed me the kitchen area, storage spaces, the geyser, electricity meter, garbage disposal method, doorbell and RO water supply. Her clear instructions made it apparent that I wasn't the first tenant she was dealing with.

Though the dilemma over this place had ended, yet, my agony had no end. Her help, her explanations, and mild manners - everything was making me restless. I desperately wanted to clarify the thing that mattered the most to me. Without it, all this would be useless.

'Ma'am, what would the rent be?' I said hesitantly, literally crossing my fingers behind my back to cross this last hurdle.

Pihu smiled again, and I barely controlled my anger. I wondered what was going on in this little girl's head, because clearly, there was something cooking.

Focussing my energy back on Annu, I knew I could manage to pay up to five thousand rupees, but my business acumen prompted me to quote the lowest price first. I was sure this place would be out on rent for way more than that, but I had to keep in mind my expenses too. I planned to check the facial expression of the landlady for the degree of displeasure this question had brought, and then decide if I needed to exponentially increase the bid.

'I think three thousand rupees is sufficient rent...' came Pihu's sweet, low voice from right next to Annu. I don't know how Annu reacted, because I myself was quite taken aback. I could not even fake a smile this time, because it was so embarrassing to say that price out loud. Three thousand rupees for an entire floor of a semi furnished flat in the heart of the city was a very poor joke!

Annu glared at Pihu now. Then rolled her eyes to look at me.

'I could pay five thousand...' I increased my bid. I didn't want my quoted price to get me thrown out of the flat.

'No issues, sir. Pay as much you can afford,' Pihu offered magnanimously. I wondered who was taking the call here. Annu could only look at me, smile and nod in affirmation. I couldn't help but think what Pihu had told her mother to get this done from her. Was she blackmailing her or something? Because it wasn't possible otherwise.

Then, Annu asked a horrible question. 'Why did you leave the school staff accommodation? I think most teachers have to live in the school premises only.'

I hesitated, then answered with a sigh, 'Actually, they have made it exclusive for families.'

Annu nodded. She had accepted my excuse and had no doubt on my intentions. For the first time ever, my bachelorhood was used for the right reason, and that too, in front of two females.

She shared her number, saying, 'Please do not hesitate to call me if you need any sort of help.' Her thin lips curved into a charming smile.

This had to be my lucky day. A great flat for minimal rent, a beautiful landlady who was polite, and the gorgeous woman's phone number, which she shared herself. I was smiling to myself at the way things were going, when I noticed that although Annu had started towards the stairs to the first floor, Pihu was still in the sitting room with me. And I had no idea why she kept looking at me like that and smiling.

'Pihu, come fast... I can't keep lunch waiting any longer,' Annu called from the stairs.

'Mom, I want to help sir,' the girl shouted back.

'Come on, Pihu! It will delay your medicine,' Annu tried to reason, and not very calmly.

'Don't bother, Pihu. I don't have much luggage. I will manage. You go on! Your mom's waiting.'

'Relax sir! I am okay.'

Pihu seemed too sweet and helpful. I mean, who lies for a stranger, rather a favourite teacher and offers a part of their home for negligible rent? She was asking how she could be of help, so I gave her a bag to unpack which had all my books. I was, after all, a teacher. But the collection did not reflect what I am trying to portray. I had only a few mathematics books, one physics book, and an entire load of erotica. I realised I shouldn't have taken the risk, but now it was too late.

As Pihu was stacking the books, she picked one and read out the title, *'Fifty Shades of Grey*...! I have heard a lot about this book. Can I borrow it for reading?' she chirped.

A teenager was asking my permission to read *Fifty Shades of Grey*. I would have given it. What if her mom got to know that her so-called maths teacher was giving out books related to biology? You know what I mean!

'No.' I said instantly, and then calmed myself a bit to add, 'I mean, you have your board exams coming up. I think you need to focus on your studies more.'

She did not seem to take any offense. I don't think she delved into the matter much, for her next question was, 'How do you find my mom?'

Completely unrelated, irrelevant and quite irrational! But the question made me think back on how much porn sites earned from 'hot mom' videos. Pihu's mom was straight out of the furnace, scintillating hot!

'Your mom is very helpful and efficient, Pihu. Manages things quite commendably,' I replied out loud, putting the demon in my head to rest.

Hearing that, Pihu hugged me. To say I was shocked would be an understatement. I had not expected it at all, and though it seemed like a reflex action from her side, I was quite uncomfortable.

'Thanks for coming here, sir.'

It was an embarrassing situation. Here I was fantasizing about her mom, while she seemed to want to be overtly close to me. I had to insist for her to go and have her lunch with Annu, and she reluctantly agreed.

When she left the room, I had a nagging feeling that she wanted to stay back and ask more questions. But thankfully, she left.

I closed the door behind her, lest she changed her mind, and went to lie down for some time. I had been craving this time with myself ever since things went out of control the previous day. I took a deep breath and tried to analyse the day as I stared at the ceiling fan. A cunning smile lit up my face as I lay on the bed. Pihu had helped me put a neat bedsheet and pillow covers on it.

'A house with two females and a male tenant,' I thought aloud. 'The perfect plot for an erotic movie.' I kept smiling foolishly at my own thoughts. Pihu's mom kept wandering in and out of my mind.

I said with a sly smile, 'I think I really liked your mom, Pihu.'

Three

I couldn't help but feel curious about the way things were turning out. Where were the other members of the family? Who rents a part of a bungalow? Agreed, the bungalow's condition does not merit the title... but still, why? Was it for money? If yes, then they could easily find someone who would happily pay a bomb for the location and space. Why did she agree to such a low rent? Just because I am Pihu's favourite teacher? That doesn't sound too convincing. And that girl is another dilemma. Why am I her favourite teacher? I don't think I have ever taught her. Actually, it was absurd the way both mother and daughter kept staring at me. Did they suspect something?

My mind was teeming with questions, but my financial incapability to afford an expensive flat had killed the mushrooming Sherlock Holmes inside me.

It had barely been a couple of years that I joined this school. There were not many people whom I could call friends. Since some of my acquaintances worked at the school, they would not want to indulge me after what had happened. I wouldn't be surprised if they started ignoring me in order to save their own jobs.

However, there was a huge number of girls who I was 'friends' with. Most of those beauties had enjoyed many evenings with me, drinking each other in pleasure. But the more I gulped, the thirstier I got.

Sometimes I wondered how in the world I had ended up making so many girlfriends! Was it my slim fair face with chocolate brown eyes, the sharp nose, and the full lips which could expertly arouse any woman, or my sense of humour, or just the charm that worked its magic?

But all that apart, true friendship and camaraderie would have remained a mystery, if not for Aarav. He was the one guy who could cheer me up in a minute, and make every moment better by just being there. He made me feel a little more human. You see, I have a different method of making friends. Quite naturally, the hottest topic of discussion I love to indulge in rarely evoked the same level of interest in people. Some would enjoy the topic, some would pretend to like it, and some would outright tell me off, but no one could discuss it with as much pleasure as I did. To my luck, Aarav was chosen because he was excellent in the same topic, and our frequencies matched to the last bit.

Our discussions were quite exciting. I narrated stories about how I seduced women, how I touched them and drove them wild, initiating a need in them which until then was unknown even to them. Aarav loved to hear and imagine those stories. Initially, he was only interested in how I did it. You know, find women who would consent, make them fall for me and like me enough to explore, the works, etc. As time passed and we became closer, I understood that he too was a slave of those needs. Honestly, I am sure everyone has these needs, but perhaps *our* inner demons were stronger than the angel.

Which reminded me, I had to be in school the next day, and Aarav was the only one who could give me any internal information now. I would be treated like an untouchable, the sick perpetrator, I was sure, despite the fact that the allegations against me had not yet been proved. I closed my eyes and hoped for things to turn better the next day.

▼

Aarav and I were sitting in the school staff cafeteria. It was right next to the students' canteen, but still segregated in a way that students couldn't disturb us, though the staff members could have a glimpse of the students sitting in the canteen.

'Wow… You lucky dog! You have shifted in a house with two women!' Aarav let out a wistful sigh while sipping his coffee.

I was trying hard to maintain a serious demeanour, because my happiness could be misunderstood as my callous attitude in the face of such a serious allegation. Though I was sure my chest had increased two sizes; swelled in pride at the task I had accomplished. Aarav's eyes showed he had understood the depth of my achievement. After all, true friends – who enjoy the same level of horniness in life, and can find something horny in the most mundane of things – understand the intention behind the other's action.

'I don't know yaar! I could get lucky, who knows.' I looked at my friend and added with a strange expression, 'But I am more worried than excited.'

'Why are you worried?' Aarav asked casually, his mouth full of the big samosa bite he had just taken.

'It's all so weird, don't you think? Suddenly a student offers me help, does all the convincing, and for a mere few thousands, I am living in an entire ground floor of a semi-furnished house in one of Pune's most posh areas!'

'What's weird about it?' I stared at him. How could he miss the point!

'Everything, man! Can't you see?' I shook my head in confusion, placing the tea cup on the table. 'I am sure there's something fishy. Something doesn't add up. The way both of them look at me, that's scary sometimes. The mother and daughter scan me like I am the last man on earth. And the way this girl keeps smiling all the time, I think she is up to something.'

Aarav guffawed at my reaction and waved off my worry. He gurgled in pleasure, 'Perhaps both of them are hungry for you.'

'No yaar. I know when a woman's stare is hungry. With them, there is something strange in the way they look at me. I can understand…' I said thoughtfully, '…Pihu is an immature teenager, so maybe she thinks I am her favourite teacher, and she is smitten or whatever. But why would her mother behave like that?'

'Who is an immature teenager? What was the name you took?' He left his coffee and samosa mid-air.

'Pihu,' I said casually.

'That childish girl from tenth standard?' Aarav almost spat that out as an insult.

'How do you know her?'

'I taught her English in eighth standard,' Aarav stated.

'Oh! How was she in studies?'

'Pathetic! She wasn't even regular to school, leave aside studying.'

'Ah! Any idea why she was irregular?'

He thought for a while and said, 'Not sure. I think she was unwell. Her class teacher would know better, if you want to know more.'

'That's weird.' I was left even more confused. 'Annu is so... confident, looks efficient and seems like she has a good understanding with her daughter. How can she allow her daughter to be so messed up? No attendance, failing board exams, not paying attention to studies, and be so reckless as to invite strangers to live in their home...?' My head was spinning with questions.

'Mr Maths teacher! Stop applying your logic to things that don't affect you! Not every problem has a solution,' he put the empty cup on the table and wiped his hands.

'Yeah... you are right,' I nodded grimly and finished off my tea as well.

'I have a bad news.' He said hesitantly and looked at me in the eyes. 'You have been summoned by the School Disciplinary Committee on Saturday. They asked me to convey it to you. I think they have issued a formal letter, but did not have an address they could send it on.' He handed me the summons.

'Bloody pricks! They have already thrown me out of the school premises. Now this... Disciplinary Committee!' I fumed. 'Did someone complain about me?' I looked at Aarav, trying to understand who could have backstabbed me like this.

'Not sure... Ananya's parents might have.'

29

Four

There are three kinds of students that a teacher comes across – the studious, the creative ones who are not good in studies, and the third, who are neither studious nor creative, but have a huge ego. Ananya belonged to the last category.

She came from a wealthy, affluent family and was quite dominating in her peer group. I had seen her participating in many cultural functions in school, and also found her to be excessively pushy, but had not paid much attention to her earlier. It was only when Aarav told me that she had suddenly become taller and gained a few cup sizes that we noticed her. Inevitably, the change in her skirt length had been inversely proportional to her height.

I remember the day clearly, as if it was just yesterday. I was teaching Tangent and Parabola in class, and Ananya sat on the front seat. I had been noticing from the corner of my eye that she had a playful smile while I taught. Not getting into it in front of an entire class, I assigned a question to the students and started walking in the aisle to assess their understanding of the topic. While gliding my gaze through the notebooks, my eyes suddenly fell on a naked thigh. I halted in my tracks. I was taking a slower and longer second look, when suddenly the owner of the long legs turned towards me. Our eyes met. I am not sure what went on inside her head or if she had seen me checking her out, but she smiled. It was not the respectful smile of an innocent student that I was used to. It was a smile which said she knew what I had been up to. Ananya did not bother to pull down her skirt, not even an inch. I had to gather myself; this couldn't be happening in my workplace.

I lost focus from Parabola and my Tangent got some signal, despite my trying real hard to save the situation.

I somehow managed to wrap up the class and leave, almost hurrying towards the staff room.

That night, I got a text message that put me in panic.

Hi Sir! Ananya this side.

As per school policy, every teacher had to share their number with the students, especially during exams, in case the students had some last-minute queries. A lot of my students also had my contact number and used to ping me on WhatsApp several times when they had queries. It was not difficult to manage them, as I could reply at convenience and it was no hassle. But this message was not the same.

I smiled at the text. The animal inside me had received the whiff of the starter. I was a pro in these rituals. I had had numerous such experiences in the past, and could well anticipate what was to come.

Hi Ananya! How are you, I replied, almost immediately.

I am good sir…

31

We went on chit-chatting, talking about her preparation for exams and other such things. I did not leave my phone for even a second and replied to every message promptly.

After wandering in several mathematical and mundane lines, she finally wrote, *Sir, I need your help to understand exponential curves ;) ;)*

Really? I am available for help any time. It would be my pleasure, I replied without any emojis, but the message was loud and clear.

I knew this was off limits. But my mind and body had understood something beyond the boundaries of school, books, student and a teacher. And mind you, I wasn't looking at changing this into an opportunity for the inner demon. Mostly, I was just having a good time, giving some fuel to my furtive imagination. She was seventeen, an age where she wanted to tread the forbidden paths. Or maybe she had already tasted the forbidden fruit and wanted some more variety. Anyway, I knew where I had to stop, for my own sake more than hers, and wanted to make the most of it.

That night, we chatted on WhatsApp for the longest time. Honestly, there were a few discussions about maths and her queries, but many related to curves. She was smart, and I made sure I wrote nothing that could go against me. It was a calculated move.

That day onwards, chatting on WhatsApp became an everyday ritual. She pinged me with some maths problem, but always led the conversation to something more interesting.

With each passing day, more and more of her thighs started showing in class. It was like offering blood to a thirsty shark.

What added misery to my woes was that the shark had been hungry since a year. I knew I couldn't indulge her too much, but my imagination went wild every night while I chatted with her, and it took all the effort of the world to keep that out of my words.

One day, she asked for my permission to come to my staff residence. I said no. A clear no, because we were not supposed to meet students in our house, leave aside girl students.

Sir, can you give me Maths tuitions? I am really not able to get the concepts. Her message seemed innocent.

Sometimes it's an advantage being a mathematics teacher.

No, it's not allowed, I typed back.

She did not reply, but instead sent a few pouting smileys. It made me feel like I was the only maths teacher left in this universe.

But you can come to me with your doubts after class tomorrow, or at home for doubt clearance once or twice, if absolutely necessary.

She sent many flying kiss emojis to that.

The chat ended, but not my imagination. When I put the phone aside, a particular body part made its presence felt a little too obstinately. It was not a comfortable reminder, and I was not sure how things would turn out.

I can never forget the day Ananya set her feet in my house. It was the school preparatory break, just before the half-yearly examinations.

There was a knock at my door. Courtesy our previous night's chat, I knew who was on the other side. I opened the door with a polite smile.

Ananya stood at the door, with her mom. She was wearing a pair of relaxed fit jeans and a bright pink polo neck t shirt. She did not look anything like she looked in school, and I wondered why she looked so different, so mellow. I realised, her previous extra curves were courtesy padded wired bras perhaps. I looked at this un-seductive avatar of Ananya. She looked like a decent, studious girl, extremely concerned about her muddled up maths concepts. And the reason of her soft appearance stood right behind her.

'Hi sir! Meet my mom,' Ananya introduced us, half-turning towards the lady behind her and smiling.

Ananya's mom seemed to be in her forties. Wearing a green and yellow salwar-kameez that covered her from neck to toe, she was slightly shorter than Ananya.

'Hello ma'am, how are you?'

'I am fine, sir. Thank you,' she said politely and I gestured at them to come in.

It often made me wonder whether her mom would still call me sir if she knew what her daughter and I had been up to. Well, perks of the profession perhaps.

Ananya's mom continued as they stepped in, 'Thank you, sir. Anaya is your fan. She always talks about you and praises you for the way you painstakingly clear her doubts.'

'Thank you for the appreciation,' I smiled benevolently, looking at Ananya and nodding in acknowledgement.

I led them into the sitting area, which had four wooden chairs placed around a small wooden table. The house was not luxurious, but it had the basics in place. The living room was of a comfortable size for a bachelor. The cooler and water filter made life easier in the heat. One portion off the wall had a small shelf to be used as the cooking area, with some storage space carved around it. I had a gas connection and managed quite well with the few available utensils for cooking. On the left was a door which led to the small but comfortable bedroom with an attached toilet. The place was small, but presentable, and extremely convenient for me. Since I had to live alone, I did not mind it too much.

'Would you like to have some water?' I offered.

Both of them politely declined.

I treated Ananya's mom in a way that was sure to make her feel that her presence was a special privilege for me. I took special care of her comfort. After all, I did not want her judging me wrongly, albeit, in a way, I wasn't being right with her daughter.

'Sir, Ananya is a very hard-working girl. Poor child is concerned about her marks in maths,' Ananya's mother requested. 'I have seen her sweat it out on her books, but somehow falls short. We are not maths experts and don't understand how best we can help her.' She looked at her hands and said hesitantly, '…If you could provide her regular tuitions, it would help her a lot.' She had spoken in fluent English and was hesitating to put forth the idea because parents knew it wasn't allowed, as per school management rules.

While she spoke, I figured she hailed from Karnataka. I could hear the Kannada accent quite clearly in her English. The gold she wore, her rings, and her clothes made it amply clear that she came from a well to do family.

'I would have been happy to teach Ananya, ma'am. She is a brilliant student and can do much better with a little guidance,'

I proclaimed like a saint who was starving himself for the welfare of life on earth. 'But school rules do not allow that. I hope you understand.' I did not even once look at Ananya. I had my rules in place. I deliberately avoided giving her any attention.

Ananya's mom nodded, understanding the arrangement. 'Sir, Ananya told me she has some problem in understanding geometry. You know, half-yearly exams are scheduled for next week. It would be immense help if you could spend some time with her.' Ananya's mom touched Ananya's jeans-clad thighs in concern.

'Well, since you are already here, I think I could give a few hours today,' I said, and imagined myself growing like a hero in her mother's eyes.

'Thank you, sir. Thank you so very much for agreeing,' Ananya's mother said and I could see Ananya's ear to ear smile from the corner of my eye.

I waved the gratitude off with my hand and smiled.

'I have a previous engagement, so I will leave you two to study. I will return in two hours to pick her up,' she offered.

Two hours! Two hours! *Two hours!* She said it once, but I heard it thrice in my head. Two hours. I had already started reviewing Ananya's thighs.

'Mom, isn't it really nice of sir to agree to help me! I want to make the most of this opportunity. I will give you a call when we are done.' Ananya looked at her mother with innocent gratitude.

Her words added fuel to my desire. This girl was something else. If she could talk like that in front of her mother, I wasn't sure what was going to happen in the two hours.

Ananya's mom nodded in agreement and took her leave. When she turned to Ananya to say goodbye, Ananya was already unpacking her bag and pulling thick books out. The concerned mother left her little girl in my safety.

I shut the door behind her to face the quiet in the room. The silence was filled with an anticipation that had nothing to do with learning difficult mathematical concepts.

Keeping a check on my breathing and voice getting husky, I said, 'Let's see what problems you are facing.'

Ananya took a deep long breath and said, 'Yeah sure.'

Five

Though the breaths had reached another level, heat in the room crossing all measure, nothing happened in our first private meeting. Yes, there were more to come.

I was on my guard, very sure that she was my student and too young to know what this could lead to. I had enough food for my horny thoughts from this meeting and her double meaning questions, which I evaded. I was sure she would not want any more than this and we could continue our little game on chats.

But the first meeting's apparent failure did not discourage Ananya. Her mom sat through the second session, waiting for almost an hour for her daughter to get done, but stopped accompanying her after that session. Perhaps Ananya got her discomfort with maths from her mother. The frequency of her doubt sessions increased, leading to our friendship becoming freer.

Now that she came alone, I made a few protocols for her. It was absolutely essential to follow them to the T if she wanted to continue coming over. She had to wear a helmet when she came, so that no one would recognise her. She could not come late in the evening. If she happened to meet anyone and was asked what she was doing in the staff colony, she was to say she had come to return my books. It all looked quite easy to manage.

I clearly remember it was a Saturday in January. I had just finished having lunch that I had cooked myself. Pune is not very cold in winters, rather quite hot in the daytime. I turned off the cooler that had been running while I had been cooking.

The house was so quiet, I could hear the clock ticking. A relaxed lunch had put me in a mellow mood and I was feeling indulgent. I dug out a small chocolate from the refrigerator and took it to the bedroom. I lay down and covered myself up to the chest. I bit into the chocolate, the aphrodisiac starting to work wonders. As it melted in my mouth, its softness reminded me of those milky, white thighs and got me high. I was enjoying the visuals my brain was showing, and I was well prepared to please myself with them this lazy afternoon. My brain and the rest of my body were working in unison too, totally in sync, when I heard a knock on my door. It was like a stop button that had put everything on halt immediately. With extreme difficulty, I carried myself to my door.

'Hi Ananya, how are you?' I said on seeing the visitor.

She was wearing a short lavender-coloured skirt, with a mustard deep V neck top. I could see her legs, and cleavage – not a very comfortable combination for the state I was in. On close inspection, I realised her cup sizes had increased again. I was happy at the visual candy in front of my eyes, but not about her visit. Half-yearly exams were over, and the presence of a student who was wearing such clothes would not go unnoticed.

'Can I come in?' Ananya asked, her eyes wide.

39

I was so engrossed in checking her out that I forgot we were still at the door.

'Yes, please,' I quickly turned, making way for her. I left the door open, just to avoid sending out any wrong signals to the few passersby.

She made herself comfortable in one of the chairs, while I excused myself and went to the washroom to splash some water on my face. I looked into the small wall mirror, preparing myself for the upcoming task. By the time I came back to the living room, Ananya was covered in sweat. She was fanning herself with a newspaper, and the door of the house was closed.

'It's so hot today, sir. I can barely breathe here.'

I felt embarrassed when she said that and offered her to come to the other room, as the fan was more effective there and the cooler threw direct air.

She left the chair and stepped into the room as I switched the cooler on. She was not at all nervous. Casually, she walked into the room and sat on my bed.

'How was your maths exam?' I asked, standing at the door.

She made a face. 'I did not do well. The questions you gave for practice, none of them were asked in the exam.'

'I had not set your paper.' I shrugged.

'Oh…!' The extrovert Ananya went silent.

'Don't be too disheartened. I might set the final examinations question paper.'

The smile reappeared on her face.

'Your exams just ended. You should take a break. Anyway, which topic do you wish to study today?'

'Algebra.' She placed the book on her lap and turned the pages.

My eyes travelled up her smooth bare thighs. They glowed as an effect of some lotion and worked their magic.

I looked at the page she had opened and pointed at a question. 'What is the value of X here, in this question?' I pointed one finger at the book and accidentally touched her leg.

A sensation ran throughout my body. Her cool body and extra soft shiny skin were testing my limits, inviting me to lose myself. She just closed her eyes and drew in a deep breath. When she reopened her eyes, all I could hear was, 'I am feeling too hot here. I will remove my top. Is that okay, sir?'

Ananya looked at me with meaningful eyes, and before I could utter a single syllable, she had pulled her top off. Her bra straps were peeping from behind her spaghetti straps. Her cups had swollen a few more millimetres, willing the fine straps to be torn off. Ananya turned to me. She looked at me, her eyes thirsty.

I stood frozen.

'Sir, I am fed up with theories. Could you please explain problems with practical examples?'

'There is no practical in maths,' I managed to say.

She looked at me like a hungry dog. Her breathing was strained when she asked, 'How do we insert a tangent around a parabola?'

I did not move an inch. This was not how it was supposed to go. Something stopped me in my tracks, and even killed the raging demon inside me. I realized she was too immature to understand the difference between love and lust, and experimenting with her sexuality at such a tender age.

I turned my face away from her and said sternly, 'Ananya, you are not allowed to come here for anything now.'

Six

DAV School had a reputation for its strict rules and regulations. They emphasised on maintaining transparency between students, parents and teachers. They held compulsory parent-teacher meetings on last Fridays of each month.

This time around, the prospect of the meeting had me in lumps. What if Pihu's Mom got a whiff of the actual reason behind my leaving the school accommodation! I was stressed beyond measure.

One, I was already under the radar and had to appear before the disciplinary committee, and two, I did not want to leave this mansion which had been suddenly bestowed on me by the heavens. That too, almost for free.

I was aware of the realities of life. I knew Annu could rent the portion out to anyone, any day, with manifold the rent that I had agreed to pay. And that's why, to tell you the truth, I had not even unpacked any of my bags fully. I had stayed tough on myself and had made up my mind for anything that came.

I had been regretting the actions of the past days. I regretted every second the way things had turned out, the way I had led her on, and how it had climaxed into my own downfall. But still, the regret has not changed me much. It was sheer foolishness, and more than feeling sorry, I was kicking myself for my carelessness.

I jumped out of my wits when there was a knock at the door.

Fearing that it could be Annu, I began arranging around the house. A bachelor's pad has many things lying around which need to be hidden – dirty underwear, a smelly sock with tiny holes in it and god knows what all. In my case, I needed to hide both. Didn't want my landlady to start regretting her decision of giving this place out to me.

I tried to hide my irritated sigh on opening the door. 'Hi Pihu! How are you?'

She barged in before I could ask her to enter. This was unexpected from a child her age. I mean, wasn't this basic etiquette. And I often wondered how Annu's child could be so unlike her sophisticated and well-mannered mother. I found it extremely rude. Height of insolence! Alright, the house belongs to her, but entering my room like this was preposterous.

'May I come in, sir?' she asked, walking in.

I was still standing at the door. 'You are already inside the house, Pihu.'

'Oh, thank you, sir.' She smiled, showing me most of her teeth.

Soon after, I got another glimpse of her immaturity. She went straight to sit on the chair in the sitting room, wearing a bright yellow pair of cotton shorts. Her bamboo thin, unattractive legs failed to draw my attention. I silently thanked the heavens above for making her so average looking.

But despite all that, her sitting in my home like that was worrying me. I left the door wide open and kept a safe distance from her. I had already been awarded the title of "the sexually abusing teacher".

'Pihu, I think you should not be coming here in the absence of your mom.' I stood with my hands across my chest and told her quite seriously.

'But why?' she counter-questioned me, as if I had taken away her birth rights.

It was not something that needed to be explained to a seventeen-year-old, I thought. I sometimes felt, girls got this knowledge instinctively. And more so, parents of today are quite prompt with such education – good touch, bad touch, staying out of trouble, not meeting strangers, not going to the paying guest when no one else was home, you know! But how could I make her understand. She had no rational mind, it seemed.

Seeing no way out of her wide eyes staring at me questioningly, I said it out loud, pointing out the obvious, 'Your coming here might displease your mother.'

'Why?' she asked genuinely taken aback. 'What are we doing here that's wrong?'

Frankly speaking, there was nothing wrong, but you know where I was coming from!

She was lost in her own treasure hunt, it seemed. She was going through the many books I had lined on the shelf. 'So many books, sir! You've read all of these?' She looked at them in wonder.

'I am a teacher,' I stated.

'I know,' there was an artless smile on her face.

A solemn face always hides the disturbances of the mind. Looking at her going through my stuff with forced calm triggered a doubt. She was searching for something in the room.

'Are you looking for something?' I asked her finally.

She looked around, hoping the thing she was looking for would appear. 'I can't see a family photo.'

Someone had spoken about my family after so long. For a moment, I wondered if I had a family. In fact, in my entire description about my life, I have not once detailed anything about my family.

I rushed the thoughts out of my mind and asked her softly, 'Why? Is it compulsory for everyone to have a family photo in their house?'

'Yes. I have seen them in all my friends' houses,' she chirped innocently.

I realized once again that it was futile to reason with her. She was persistent, and closed her ears while talking, it seemed. So she went on and on.

'You have come here to ask about my family photo?' I was getting exasperated now, and wanted her to leave.

'No!' she smiled and sat back on the chair. Reluctantly, I rested my back on the wall opposite her.

She suddenly straightened her back in excitement and asked me, 'Do you believe in angels?'

I could not understand how to deal with her.

'You have come here to ask that?' This time I was rude.

'No, I wanted to show you something,' she said with the same level of excitement.

She smiled from ear to ear and fished out a phone from her pocket. 'I got a new phone. I wanted you to see it.'

I picked the phone and turned it around. 'An iPhone!' I pretended I was impressed and faked interest in the thing. But inside my head, I was wondering, does a class tenth girl require such an expensive phone? Knowing that asking that question could get me into a long, unrelated answer, I rather asked, 'What is the specialty of this phone?'

'Sir, it has a new 6-core GPU which is fifty percent faster than the other phones. The headphone jack has helped Apple make its new iPhones slimmer and boost its battery life too. It also has stereo speakers, you know. It has all the latest apps, beautiful interface and it's so light weight,' she rattled off.

It was hard to believe she was aware of all that. The way she usually spoke left a very juvenile impression of her, and this was quite surprising. That was the first time I thought she might have some brains.

I raised my eyebrows to show I was impressed. 'Wow, it definitely is a nice phone. Any other special feature?' I asked coldly.

The girl who had appeared intelligent just a few seconds back said something which failed a lifetime of analysis. She said, 'Yes, you can make phone calls too.'

Seven

What will happen to my job? I hope the school does not issue a termination letter. Will they give me a negative character certificate? Will I be allowed to offer an explanation or something, because, this time, I didn't really do what they think I did!

I was trying hard to sleep, but these thoughts plagued me and kept me awake. I kept tossing and turning in bed, which squeaked a couple of times

Ever since Aarav had told me that I had been summoned by the school disciplinary committee next Saturday, I had been panicking. I wondered why Ananya would complain about me! For not doing anything? Ridiculous! I always knew she was made of more ego than anything else, but I had not imagined in the wildest of my dreams that she could stoop so low.

The disciplinary committee of our school consisted of a bunch of frustrated souls who could not accept others' happiness. They would happily sacrifice me in the name of upholding their hollow image.

Nowadays, like most corporate giants, all established schools go for a background check of their employees. Any written black mark on the experience certificate, or even a faint mention of summons from disciplinary committee, leave aside the result of it, could ruin my life.

I had already begun looking at other schools and had updated my CV on Naukri.com. I did not want to miss any opening. It was a mess, and after all this fuss, I was convinced that *I* was solely responsible for all the unwanted troubles in my life.

I was only a year old in Pune. Like I said, I did not have many friends. When I was in staff quarters, I could go to Aarav's place anytime. Now I was in a posh colony of self-important people, who found it beneath them to interact with their neighbours. There was always a dead silence on the roads. A couple of guards strolled the length of the lane and whistled after fixed intervals, to signal that all was well. But other than that, it looked like a dead place to me.

After shifting to this posh yet dead society, when I craved friendly interaction, I missed Aarav. For me, the best part of having a crazy friend like him was that we could ride the same thoughts and reach the pinnacle of happiness, anytime. Now he wasn't around, and I did not want to bother him in the dead of the night with my fears.

I had tried speaking to Ananya, to try and convince her to take the complaint back, but I couldn't get through. Perhaps her parents had taken away her cell phone. Honestly, I never liked Ananya very much. For me, she was one of the many things I had stared at for pleasure. That's all. With her, I had done nothing, I had wanted to do nothing. I had clearly categorised her as out-of-bounds-eye-candy. No promises had been broken, no limits were crossed, so this entire fiasco was quite a shock.

It was only 11 p.m. I was awake, restless, lonely, feeling unwanted, and bogged down with fear of being jobless anytime now.

I suddenly started feeling locked down and claustrophobic. I sat up with a jerk, put on a blue T-shirt that had been hanging behind the door and came to the living area. I pulled the entrance door open and the cool weather instantly cheered me up. Thinking of taking a stroll, I walked outwards. Then I glanced at the first floor. The house seemed to be resting in darkness. I assumed both Annu and Pihu must have slept by now.

The pleasant weather was uplifting my mood. *Why the hell was I stuck with these two crazy ladies? I should go out and live!* I had the medicine which was the panacea of all the problems.

I went in and closed the door again. Assured nothing would disturb me, I opened my old mate, and poured a few drops of McDowell's No.1. The brand was my favourite. After all, I am a teacher. I couldn't possibly afford to have expensive tastes. While soft music played on my smartphone, I wet my parched throat with the golden elixir, relishing in the luxury of life. Alcohol doesn't permit one to do things better, but perhaps convinces us to be less ashamed of doing things poorly.

I had downed a couple of refills when I felt the need for some fresh air, I went out. The garden was too small for a stroll, so I thought of going to the terrace. Annu had told me I could use it at any time. I took the steps to the terrace, the bottle still clutched in one hand. With sloppy wet lips, I kissed my mate of lonely nights. Fresh air, a disposable glass, and a bottle dear to my heart! What else could a man need?

I was at the first floor landing when I heard voices. I could also see the small half-opened window and a dim light inside.

'Mom, this story was not new,' Pihu complained.

I halted in my tracks to hear the soft voices. The bed must be close to the window, I guessed, because I could hear the mother and daughter clearly. I don't know what took over me, for I sat on the floor, concentrating on the conversation between the two crazy females in my life, clutching the bottle close to my chest.

'How on earth can I tell you a new story every day?' The tired mother said softly.

'Mom, if you can only tell old stories, then tell me the story of the angel and the demon.'

'Pihu, you hear that story every day!' There was a hint of exasperation in Annu's voice.

Every day! I felt a chill. I was drunk, yes, but for a few seconds, the McDowell's lost its No. 1 spot, losing its effect. What a silly girl! Who hears the same story again and again! And I wasn't sure I knew anyone else of her age who would be listening to stories to go to sleep. I wanted to bang the precious bottle on my head.

My reverie broke when Annu started narrating the story.

'There was an angel. She wore a flowy white dress. And not too far away lived a demon, he wore a black suit.'

'Mom, why should the demon wear black every day? Change the colour today.'

Annu seemed to give the idea some thought, 'Okay… let's make it blue.'

My eyes fell on the sleeves of my blue T-shirt. The whisky's effect had nearly evaporated. I fumed silently. The demon inside me wanted to pounce on them.

I banged my palm on my head now. How on earth could a seventeen-year-old girl demand to hear a childish story! I was a teacher. I had interacted with hundreds of students of varied age. This girl was definitely weird!

Before I lost my cool completely, I sprinted to the other end of the terrace. The sight of the area was refreshing.

The Mula river flowed calmly behind the house's boundaries, glittering in the cool moonlight. With urbanisation, the river had lost its original robustness and slimmed down into a canal. Although polluted, at least there were no illegal constructions around the river and it was lush green on both the sides.

Nature's beauty, serenity of the water and the cheap whiskey had transported me. The cool air rustled the leaves of the present and lifted the dust off my past. As memories began flooding me, I couldn't help but think of my family. How bad I had been when I was a boy! I spent my entire childhood wishing I were older, and now that I was, I was thinking what I had become. I often wished I could be a child again so I could grow up once again and be whoever I wanted to be.

My father had a transferable job in the State Bank of India. We kept moving from one town to another, every few years, and had lived in many parts of the country.

Things began to change for me when we were living in Almora. I was around eight years old back then. Shifting constantly never let me make long-lasting friends, and I was bad at making friends I used to play with kids of the locality and make acquaintances, but never friends. I couldn't imagine parting from friends. So to while away time, I used to sit on my bed and look out of the window. My classes were held in the second shift, so from 7:30 in the morning, I would sit idly and watch the road. Back in those days, I did not have any greed or urge for girls. Obviously, I was too young to understand. But watching school girls passing by in their varied length skirts gave me a strange satisfaction. I always watched their legs. They were all beautiful, differently. Some were extra exposed, some exceptionally fair and some used to be hidden too much by their extra-long skirts. I don't know why, but those legs always caught my attention.

With time, the ritual to pass time became the habit of gazing at those legs. I would sit there for hours. In fact, one of my fondest memories is when a class tenth girl touched my cheek, and said, "...you are really cute." It had taken me a few hours to fall asleep that night. The touch had been on the cheek, but she had unintentionally woken something else in me. I failed to recognise this demon raising its head at that time. After all, I was only ten years old.

My childhood was not luxurious, but I always had the things that I needed. I was a demanding child, and my parents did all in their might to fulfil those demands. I was closer to my father than my mom. In fact, I often visited the bank he worked at. I was very proud of my father because of what he did. I understood only this much that people purchased everything with money, and at the bank, I saw them lining up in front of my father. I thought my father was the owner of all that money. I used to think, he was the richest man on this earth. That's why I used to get surprised, whenever my expensive demands were turned down with some excuse or the other. Reality dawned on me quite late in life.

We were a small family of four members. While mom and dad were okay, there was a villain in my life. Born several years before me, he remained buried in books all the time, which made my life hell. It's not that I hated him from birth. But there was a chorus which was sung to me all my life – 'Look at your brother. How good he is!'

He was favoured and appreciated all the time. For studies, for being so humble, for being sincere, and mostly because he never demanded anything. I started hating him for these reasons. I was befuddled, how could anyone be good in studies! Now that I look back, I feel it was more a result of the constant comparison by others. And my brother, he always praised me. I never realized how wrong I was in judging him, until it was too late.

I failed to clear the convent school's entrance test, but my brother got through. I had always dreamt of studying with those girls in short skirts. And now, my brother would be living my dream, though he had no interest in whether the girls came in skirts or jute bags.

It's the irony of life. The more you want a thing, the greater the force with which the universe drives it away. I finally took admission in an average school, about a kilometre away from my brother's. I would accompany him and just watch those naked legs for a few minutes before heading to my own school.

As time passed, my over-studious brother cracked DCE, the Delhi College of Engineering, and we all shifted to Delhi. I had to change my school again. And again had to hear the same old song - 'Look at your brother! He has always been brilliant in studies, hardworking, and now it has paid off.'

I offered flowers to god and thanked him that my brother had not cleared IIT. Else, my family would have made my life living hell.

I went to my brother's engineering college twice, out of curiosity, and he never said no. I found, there were no attractive girls in his batch. Moreover, he had taken mechanical engineering. It was a bunch of guys, immensely happy in their own world. And if, by mistake, they found one beautiful girl, the entire college would start hovering around her.

I lost my desire to become an engineer completely after seeing the sorry state of these boys. But I belonged to a middle-class family and these things are not our decisions totally. So my father forced me to fill the IIT JEE form, among many other useless exams. But my rank could not secure me a seat. Naturally, without inclination, hard work or miracles, there was no way I could get in. Finally, I took admission in Jagan University to do B.Sc.

My family was depressed beyond consolation. Jagan University failed to please them, and so did their younger son. They complained, blaming me for breaking the chain and not following the great Indian path of doing engineering. My life had not found its significance!

I was upset, and almost scared to come home, but at least I had the drive to pursue my education. After a childhood of struggle, I finally found my freedom and happiness in Jagan University.

Eight

I was tidying up my room and putting things in their right places the next morning, when there was a knock at the door. I wasn't a great enthusiast for neatness, but I also didn't like a messed up home, so managed to do the bare minimum. I waited to finish with the sheet that I was folding, but the door was knocked again after a few seconds, and then again. With each passing second, the knocks were getting intensified. I half assumed it was Pihu and wanted to delay seeing her, even if by a bit.

'Neel sir! Are you there?' a voice called out.

It was Annu. I hollered, 'Just a second, Annu ji,' walking towards the door.

I opened the door. Pihu was indeed there, grinning. Annu wore a comfortable light brown kurti and dark culottes. She looked nice in this simple ensemble too. I could see the stiff pleats of her kurti. Well, she always dressed smart.

Looking at Pihu reminded me that this beautiful woman was a single mother. I was curious to know the story behind this big bungalow and her marital status. I invited her inside, but she refused.

The three of us stood silently. Finally, Annu spoke, 'Sorry, but are we disturbing you, sir?'

'Nothing important, Annu ji,' I behaved as if I had been called away from solving the biggest mystery of mankind.

'Sir, this is a form that I need you to fill,' Annu waved some paper in front of my face.

'What is this form for?'

'Police verification... basic information of tenants.'

'Oh!' I said, nodding. More of a formality. She had come as a landlord. I took the papers from her and assured her, 'I will fill them and return in some time.'

'Thank you. I have something else to ask. If you don't mind, can you please tell me for how many days are you planning to stay?'

I thought over my response, and she stood there looking at me. She would not leave without getting an answer, I was sure. She looked at me in the same weird way that Pihu did, and it made me shift my weight from one foot to another. Didn't they have anything else to do in life? Their joint gaze was quite unsettling.

I shrugged. 'Maybe six months... Is there any concern?' I was not sure if I would retain my job for six months or not. Still, I dared to give a tentative timeline.

'That is great!' Pihu screamed gleefully with a winner's smile.

Great! Why would she respond like that? This girl was absolutely beyond me.

'How are you managing your food, sir?'

'I cook,' I said with a confident smile this time.

'Great!' Annu said.

The mother and daughter were playing some game of greatness. I needed to distract them for this endless great saga to end.

'Thanks. So, where do you work, Annu ji?'

'I work in Polaris Hospital, Wakad. I am the head of the nursing staff there.'

So that was the secret of her fitness, and why she cared about my comfort and food. It was instilled in her because of her profession.

'I have a request to make, sir.' Annu started a bit hesitantly, and I nodded. 'Usually, I drop Pihu to school every morning.' She looked at me with eyes of an overworked mother. 'Will it be possible for you to accompany Pihu to school today?'

Pihu looked like she was dying to go to school. She was blushing like an overripe pumpkin which could blast with happiness any moment. I could see her obsession for me. I desperately wanted to refuse. My situation was bad enough due to Ananya, and Pihu was going to be an unnecessary trouble. But then, I was acutely aware of the rent I was paying for this place was insufficient. The favour had created an obligation for me.

Before I could say anything out loud, Annu said, 'There is no obligation, sir.'

'No... no Annu ji. Not a problem,' I told her promptly.

There were bright smiles on both their faces. She was preparing to leave for the hospital, but I stopped her for a while to ask, 'I need to fill the form and details of the house, Annu ji. Can I know the name of the owner of this house, please?' I said looking at the form.

'This property is on my name...' was all that she had said when her voice was drowned under that of the main gate bell.

Annu walked up to the gate and opened it. 'Hi, Dr Vedant! Good morning...'

Pihu was still standing with me. The girl who until now had been smiling for no reason had suddenly become sad. She did not even go to greet the guest. I knew she was strange, and this added to my doubts. It also scared me that she had this special feature of weirdness only for me. I thought of confirming.

'You look upset, Pihu. Is something wrong?'

'Dr Vedant.' She said but did not even turn to look at me. As if she wanted to stare this guy down.

I guessed that he must be a frequent visitor, as Pihu knew him quite well. Could be Annu's colleague.

'But why did you get upset on seeing him?'

'Because I don't like him.'

Annu returned with Dr Vedant, 'Vedant, this is Neel sir, our new tenant.'

Vedant and I greeted each other. Despite what I felt about Pihu, I tried to understand what could be bothering her.

'Pihu, go get ready, fast! You wouldn't want Neel sir to get late because of you,' Annu instructed her daughter before she left for the hospital with Vedant.

Pihu and I were left alone now.

'Why don't you like him?' I don't know why I was curious.

'Because he is a doctor and he comes often and...' she hesitated.

'And?' I prodded.

'He asks mom out for dinner dates and coffee dates, without me.'

I could sense Pihu felt left out, which would have been okay in a ten or twelve-year-old, but at seventeen...?

'You should not be complaining, Pihu. Your mom is a grown up woman. She knows what she is doing, and if she is going alone with him, it means, maybe she likes him.'

'No, she does not like him!' Pihu said with a certain confidence that surprised me.

'Then why would she go out with him?'

'Because he is a good doctor.'

Nine

The not so awaited Saturday was finally here.

I had been summoned by the vigilante – the disciplinary committee.

The uncomfortable bench was pinching my behind, and making waiting all the more stressful. I had been waiting for nearly an hour, and had nothing to do but wait. It was like waiting to be slotted into heaven or hell, after being butchered brutally. I felt like a sacrificial lamb.

A peon came towards me. 'Sir, they are calling you inside.'

I was not sorry to leave the bench, but it took me some effort to take the next steps.

It was a full house. Eleven teachers, including three women, sat behind the long table. I knew for a fact that some of these were those useless teachers who had little to teach in their subject, so had voluntarily taken the moral responsibility of an entire generation. I had seen some of them waste their entire time in school in studying which girl was roaming around with boys, whose skirt was too high, whose socks were too low, and all those details. I wasn't too sure if it was actually a part of duty to their post, or the duty to their wanton spirit.

School had ended at 2 p.m., and now, at 4 p.m., it was deserted. No one in the room seemed to be in a hurry. There was no restlessness on their faces. They all looked relaxed, as if they had all the time in the world. In fact, they were anticipating some fun, like the matinee show was about to begin.

I took the lonely chair on the other side of the long table, sitting a couple of metres away, as if I would pounce on them or kill them if I sat too close.

Without any introduction, one of the oldest among them – the principal – spoke up sternly. 'Mr Neel Kumar, we have received a written complaint that you were privately tutoring a student?'

I was shaken to the core. Is this elaborate set up only for private tuition? I assumed Ananya's parents were too big shot to let their daughter's name come up in an inquiry. Plus, naming her and putting allegations would have led to a scandal. I assumed they had refrained from those charges.

The respectable principal continued to read from a paper, 'The school rules clearly state that you are not supposed to indulge in such activities.' She looked up at me, hands joined on the table. 'Care to explain what compelled you to do so? You accept the charges, I believe.'

Charges! I gulped my own saliva. I felt as though the Chief Justice of India was about to announce a verdict against me. And the worst part, there was nobody to defend me.

'Do you accept the charges?' she raised her voice, while all others stared at me, unblinking.

'No. I don't accept them. I plead not guilty,' I spoke like a freedom fighter, refusing to surrender to the British.

'We have come to know that a female student has been coming to your room, quite often.' She finished and I could see the males of the committee smirk and pass each other sly glances.

I gathered all my patience and replied as politely as possible under the circumstances, 'Madam, I had explained everything to you the night I was asked to leave the staff quarters. I explained about Ananya. I told you she had come for doubt clearance.'

'But, the panel wants to hear from you…'

The cast was complete. The free matinee show was about to start. I took a long breath. 'Ananya had some doubts in maths; she came to my quarters with her mother to discuss some math problems. I did not charge her any money. It was a one-off consultation, without monetary privilege. It was not tuition in any way, because I did not ask for any compensation against it.'

The smirks only grew more evident. I had said the wrong word – compensation. They must have started imagining that if not cash, I must have been paid in kind. How could I be so foolish!

'Mr Neel, a student coming over even after the exams, and staying for quite long…' The statement from one of the panellists raised many sarcastic eyebrows.

I remained silent. I guessed they knew more about those hours than I did.

'Mr Neel, because of your irresponsible behaviour, other students are also demanding tuitions. There should not be any preferential treatment for anyone.'

'She was discussing the paper, because she felt she hadn't done well. But if you think that was preferential treatment, then I am sorry. I will ensure it is not repeated in future.'

'What were you teaching… biology?' One teacher mocked. The rest of them burst into laughter as though he had cracked the funniest joke. The principal and I remained serious.

The room was filled with useless jerks, who were all masters in the art of fluttering tongues to please their boss.

Unable to make me flinch, jumping from one comment to another, one teacher dared, 'Did you have sex?'

I glanced at my wrist watch. It had taken them fifteen minutes to come to the point. All this court drama and bullshit disciplinary committee! They were just interested in whether or not I had sex.

I was not going to give in, because this time, I wasn't even at fault. 'No! Why would I? I am her teacher. And how is tuition related to this in any way?'

There was an uncomfortable silence. They were not happy with my curt response.

'Is there anything else you would want to ask?' I made my displeasure clear.

'You can wait outside, Mr Neel. We will call you soon,' the principal instructed.

After some more wait on the uncomfortable bench, the verdict was announced. I had been found guilty. I wondered how and why, but then fathomed that the image of the school was far more important than a teacher like me.

I was given two choices – either I could put down my resignation, serve the notice period and leave. Or, they would terminate me with immediate effect.

The very next day, I tendered my resignation and began counting days of my notice period.

Ten

I would not receive any salary during the notice period and the additional rent had increased my expenses. It was February. Schools would close in a few days for study leave before final examinations and then there would be summer holidays. I saw no scope of getting another job before June or July. I did not have the habit of saving till then, so I was in a soup. At the most, I could manage for one or two months. But what after that?

Every time I was in crisis, I missed my only relative, my mother. We Indians have one thing in common. Rich or poor, saint or dacoit, everyone has extreme respect for their moms.

I do have a brother, who lives in Vashi, which is just about one hundred and fifty kilometres away from my place. It is easily accessible by road. But I did not have any relationship with him anymore. And I was the only one responsible for that too.

Having nobody else to go to, I booked a train ticket for Delhi for the next day, although a bit hesitant. There was an awkwardness in meeting mom also. After all, it had been a long time and I had been rather busy with my emptiness.

I informed Annu that I'd be gone a few days, and didn't miss the look on Pihu's face. Preoccupied with my own thoughts, I chose to stay quiet and left for Delhi.

The pleasure and pain of a train journey is the endless time you have on hand. But then, nothing threatens a corrupt body more than a free mind. Once settled comfortably, I started reliving my early days.

When I was in the sixth standard, I got my first school complaint. I was caught red-handed, drawing a nude picture on the desk. My then class teacher summoned my parents with a note – "Neel is involved in a serious disciplinary offense. Request the parents to come and meet Ms Meetu."

Since my father was busy at the bank, only mom accompanied me. It was outrageous when the teacher displayed my piece of art on the wood. I am not sure if they had examined my art closely, but I had attempted to carve Meetu madam's face. She was my class teacher. The delicate curves that I had shown so artfully, were an outcome of my vivid imagination. If the same picture had been made by Mr M F Hussain, someone might have paid a million dollars. But when I did it, my mom had been summoned with a complaint.

It was embarrassing, watching mom seeing those extra curves and perfect body outlines. She looked embarrassed and amazed at the same time.

Ma asked, 'This was made by Neel?'

'Yes,' Meetu ma'am confirmed.

'The art is so good. Neel couldn't possibly draw so well,' my mother commented, her eyes still on the art, quite sure her son wasn't the type who could sketch, leave aside such curves.

Good drawing! I was dying to claim it as my masterpiece. All the curves, the rise of breasts, the nipples were so perfect. It was sheer irony that the great artist was not getting his due. My blind-in-her-son's-love mom did not allow me the credit.

But Meetu ma'am confirmed I was caught red-handed and my mother had to apologise profoundly, with a request of no strict action to be taken against me, as I was just a child.

But had she really not recognised the work? I soon got my answer when on reaching home, finding an alone moment, she blasted on me. 'Neel, what is wrong with you? Why are you wasting your energy in these petty things? Get away from these distractions. One day this is going to ruin you.'

I nodded, distressed. A few minutes ago, I had believed I was M F Hussain, and now suddenly, I had become useless.

This was a mom's anger, irrelevant as usual, I felt. But everything said and done, she was the first woman who symbolized unconditional love for me. The rest have either ignored me, or misjudged me.

I don't remember if I gave my family the happy moments my brother did. They were jubilant when my brother got placed from the DCE campus in Mahindra Satyam in Noida. After the celebration was over, my father asked me, 'What do you wish to do in life?'

It was not a question; it was a taunt. I gave the question the most important few seconds of my life. 'I want to be a teacher in a convent school.'

It was strange for them. When all the aspiring teachers were dreaming of grabbing a government school job, I was the only human being who wanted to be a teacher in a convent school.

There were no perks, no extra benefits, lesser holidays, more work pressure and what not. My father did not say anything, and my mother made a face.

Since I was always under pressure to perform better, I had fallen in line with similar peers quite early on in life. I began smoking joints when I was twenty. Don't ask me how or when or why, but the entire list of my evils risks having more haters, so I stopped.

I'd often ask for money at home, making one excuse or another. My habits did not go unnoticed and my father stopped my pocket money. Can you believe it? How was I to manage my expenses? He never once sat with me to tell me where I was wrong. He never thought it worth his time to explain to me that it was okay to not be so intelligent and I could do better with my life. I felt so distraught because he had only one line to chant – '...look at your brother...'

I fell into further bad company and abused myself no end. My mother did not have much money to spare, and I was fighting my loneliness with these habits. So I started stealing things from home, which I sold.

Mom wanted to stand by me and support me, but my anger with my father was so much that I did not give her many chances to salvage me. She had rarely compared me with anyone, encouraged me to make the most of my capabilities, but I did not pay any heed to her.

Everything was fine till I was twenty-five. Our family lived together, and no matter what happened, we were there for each other. Despite my differences with my father and my ignorance of my mother's advice, my brother Nikhil always encouraged me.

He wasn't the proud one, and made sure to include me in every little event of his life. Then, he got a job in TCS Mumbai and he relocated. I too got a teacher's job in Pune, and shifted for the same. But the truth is, his job was not the only reason behind his relocating to the new place, and as for everything else that had happened in my life till then, this was also partly my doing.

Nikhil got married to Neha, who had been with him in office. Nikhil was the kind of guy who would evoke love – sincere, down to earth, very easy to talk to and quite loyal in relationships. The new addition in our family, my sister-in-law Neha, was gorgeous. She fit in as if we knew her for ages. Not just her physical beauty, but intelligence and charm were all over the place. I could not control my mind from wandering in strange thoughts on seeing such a beauty. I won't lie, I tried hard to avoid looking at her that way. After all, she was my brother's wife. But living under the same roof, it was beyond my powers to stop thinking about her.

It was New Year's eve. Mom and dad had gone to Almora to meet an old relative. Nikhil and Neha were getting ready for a party. Nikhil called out to me that they were leaving and I came to lock the door behind them. When I saw her, I was ashamed that I was her brother-in-law. She was smoking hot in her body-hugging black dress which ended at her thighs. The dress shone, but was marred by the glow on her smooth legs. I did not notice any other body part. Only the long and beautiful legs, which were extra exposed with the short dress. Those legs in high heels were all over my mind. I imagined them walking in the house. There was something magical in them. That night, looking at her like that, I officially lost it! I could think of nothing but Neha.

Her thoughts were tempting food for a hungry mind and jackpot for the pervert soul.

In thinking of her like that, I killed a relationship that day. I visualized her like a soft doll for my satisfaction. From then on, my actions changed. Her clothes, accessories, undergarments, shoes, almost everything she used held attraction for me. When she wore a saree, I could only see the uncovered portion. And then flashes of those exposed parts would accompany me all the time.

Quite naturally, Neha realized she was getting extra attention from me. After then, she caught me staring at her a couple of times.

One day, we were sitting across each other on the dining table. The evening tea was nothing when I could feast my eyes on her cleavage. She understood what I was up to, and our eyes met. I looked back at my tea cup, but she did not move an inch. That was my signal. Maybe she was finding it adventurous to indulge me.

I cannot confess more than this. She is still my brother's wife. But yes, we did explore this adventure a bit further. Double meaning talk and naughty smiles were shared, she dressed up at home, as if for me, and I did my bit by showering undivided attention on her. Our WhatsApp chat messages began with casual talk and went on to something much bolder in a matter of minutes.

One day, I was out for some work when I received Neha's message that she was alone at home. I rushed back, only to find her in the same short black dress that had changed the way I looked at her. I was not sure what she wanted, but I knew what

I was here for. Her seductive body and my uncontrollable desire gave new heights to our passion that day.

People give reasons, make excuses, and blame it on circumstances. I will not. I had tried to seduce her, and had managed to break the wall, though only a bit. We had kissed passionately and I was left high, wanting much more than that. But there was a strange reluctance at both sides. The rules of morality are not the conclusion of our excuse. Somewhere we were not ready to break everything.

After we drew apart, we were still alone. I sat on the bed while Neha went towards the washroom to change maybe. My mom would be home soon.

I was imagining how her bare body and perfect curves would feel when my eyes fell on her fat gold chain, lying unattended on the bed. I calculated the amount of money it could get me, and slowly slipped it into my pocket.

I was not stealing for the first time. After my father stopped my pocket money, I was driven to stealing from home quite often. But this was the most expensive sin, I would say. It cost me my family.

Neha and I were living in a wonderland, believing no one knew about us. She had to be extra careful and take extra efforts in hiding the love bites, because the moment we would be alone, I would give her a few more. The stolen touches, short hard kisses kept fuelling our fire.

Then, Nikhil took some days off from work. He and Neha went on a small holiday to Nainital. I don't know what happened there, but when they returned, she started avoiding me. Nikhil – the guy who had stood by me in the worst of phases in life

– started behaving rudely. I thought he knew something, but I was not sure. Neha was never alone at home after that day. Whenever Nikhil was out of town, she made some excuse and spent the night in her friends' or parents' place. And within a month from then, Nikhil got a job in Mumbai.

When they were leaving, among others' parting notes, I said, 'I will come to visit you in Mumbai.'

Neha did not say anything, but I got a firm reply from Nikhil. 'Please, don't ever come to my house.'

And I did not have the courage to ask why.

I felt bad because he had always been a soft-spoken man. His harsh reply implied that I had driven him to a point of no return. I had changed him for the worse, taking away his faith from relationships.

Eleven

Ide-boarded at Hazrat Nizamuddin railway station in Delhi and
hired an Ola cab to head to Dwarka. There was no excitement
in me to meet mom. Maybe I did not want to see her defeated
face again. And Dad, I wasn't even sure if he would want to
see me, I certainly didn't want to meet him. After all, I was the
biggest disappointment of his life; and he, mine.

The two BHK flat in Dwarka Sector 11 was sufficient for my
parents. It was not the home where we had grown up, thanks to
my father's transferable job. My father had purchased this flat
after retirement, wishing the family to stay together. My father's
greatest dream was to have a loving family that would serve as a
reward for all his hard work. Like all great dreams, this one was
also unrealistic.

I was meeting mom after nearly one year. I approached her
whenever I needed money. Occasionally, I would call my mom
to check on her health, but she called me every Sunday. This was
the uniqueness of a mother. She refused to hate even a person
like me.

They say the best medicine in the world is a mother's hug. When I hugged my mom, I forgot about everything else that was happening in life.

After asking about my health and well-being and confirming about hers, she asked, 'All well? You are coming to Delhi in February. Exams would be going on at the school right now. How did your school allow you?'

I found mom's behaviour a little different this time around. She had always welcomed me home, and not questioned why or how I had landed there.

'I was missing my mom,' I said with a smile.

'Seriously? You were missing your mom? Has something bad happened?'

'Need something bad happen for me to meet you, mom?' I asked perplexed, as she handed me a glass of water.

'Last time when you said you are missing me, you were fired from your first job.'

Moms know more than anyone. I smiled. I wanted to hug her and cry, but did not.

I asked about Nikhil and other relatives, and Mom updated me. There were happy things going on with mama, mausi and tau ji. After speaking to mom, I realized, I still had so many relatives.

I changed and ate, talking at length with mom about nothing in particular. I was really unwinding. Next evening, mom and I were watching television. As usual, my father had gone off to sleep early. It was around 10 p.m. and mom was watching some TV serials, back to back. I knew Dad was not sleeping early because of me, but because the queen of the house had the TV remote. I was not really a fan of these programmes, but was just giving her company.

'Have you spoken to Nikhil lately?' she asked me, out of the blue.

'No, Mom. He never calls...' the pause was thoughtful, '... so I don't.'

There were many unsaid things in that silence. She understood, and so did I.

'He is just two hours away from your place. At least you could try meeting him once.'

This was not the first time mom had urged me to bridge the gap that had built between us. How could I tell her that I had closed that road myself? It was awkward for me to face my loving brother after whatever had happened.

Mom's continuous chant was difficult to bear. I planned to bring up the relevant topic for which I was there.

'Mom, the school will break after exams. Since I am not a permanent faculty, they are not going to pay me—'

'Didn't you say while moving that you are joining as a permanent faculty?' she cut me short.

This is the problem with mothers. They remember way more than they should, and do not understand administrative excuses much.

'No, Mom. No work, no salary.'

'So, no salary for two months?'

'Three months.'

Understanding dawned soon after, and my loving mom asked the question I had been waiting for.

'How much money would be sufficient?'

'No clue,' I took a long breath, giving an impression that I was tensed.

I knew she wouldn't have much saved, but I also knew a source from where she could manage it.

'Let me try....'

'Are you going to ask Papa?'

'No. Papa will not be ready to give anything easily. He will have a million questions...'

'So, you are going to ask Nikhil?' I spoke as though she was compromising my self-respect.

'I am not sure if he would be willing to help you. Let's see if I can do something.'

My mother's words had so many ifs and buts, but the thing which I appreciated in mom was, she was resourceful. It was not the first time I was asking money from her. She had always arranged something for me.

I picked up the remote and switched to news channels. Randomly flipping through, I stopped at ABP News. The anchor with a dense beard was howling his lungs out – "...*sannate ko cheerti hui, sunn ker degi...*" – he was hosting the show in his signature style.

I often wondered if he was actually hired by the channel to scare people. To my sheer bad luck, today he was hosting the show on a serial rapist.

He shouted in his patent style, which was quite unpleasant to the ears, 'Meet this rapist! Radio cab driver misbehaves with a helpless lady passenger...'

How typical of my dear Delhi, I thought! Even when a dog barks, the media reports it as howling.

That's when my mother said, 'What a monster!' and I noticed this strange thing. Instead of thinking about the woman who was the victim, I was thinking of the driver. I was trying to understand his mind frame, of why he had forced himself on the lady.

I was shaken out of my thoughts, and turned to her. 'How disgusting!' my mother repeated, rattled by the news.

I changed the channel immediately. I found it very uncomfortable to watch such a thing in my mother's presence. A voice inside me poked that I had been doing a whole lot behind her back, even inside her home, then why was I so conscious now? I was stunned. I just sat back and ignored the voice of my conscience.

'I don't know why men look for forceful sexual satisfaction. This desire is so prevalent nowadays,' I spoke to my mom. She was not Aristotle or some philosopher, but she was a woman. Moreover, the woman who brought me into this world.

'Every human being has some desire, Neel. Sometimes, they can control the desire, and sometimes, the desire controls them.'

If that would have been a speech given in Europe, she could have been considered the new philosopher of the century. But she was imparting a stale theory to a son, who only understood his own desires.

'If desire is so harmless, how do you think some can control it, while others cannot?'

My mother was thinking and answering all my questions, perhaps indulging in a general discussion. The truth was, I was talking about myself. Then she asked me something.

'What do you see when you see a woman?'

Seeing me hesitate, she urged, 'You can talk to me openly, Neel. I am your mother.'

I closed my eyes. The darkness in front of them helped me share my dark thoughts. 'I see them naked. I see the body. Their thighs, legs... nipples, act as the deepest energy source.'

I snapped my eyes open, staring at my mother in sheer disbelief. I had spoken out loud like this for the first time and I was scared that she would judge me. How would I ever face my mother now, I wondered!

She considered my revelations for a few seconds, her expression blank. But when she spoke, I heard the loving mother who refused to give up on her son. 'Do you see me like that, Neel?'

'Mom, please!' I screeched, disgusted. 'How can you talk like that?'

'I am also a woman. Why have you never thought about me like that?'

'You are my mother, that's why!'

'A woman is a mother, a sister, a friend, a daughter to someone. You can understand these relationships better when you become a father or a husband. A relationship is the mother of all feelings. You will realise that she is not just a body, she is much more than that.'

▼

I had spent a couple of nice days with her and was all set to leave for Pune. I had just finished packing my bag. I did not inform papa about my departure, because he wasn't bothered.

'Neel, I will come from the ATM…'

The word "ATM" always puts a smile on my face.

Mom returned in fifteen minutes. I waited a couple of minutes for her to hand over the cash, but none came.

I said, twice, 'Mom, I am calling the taxi.'

She nodded silently, and I noticed sadness on her face. I understood, she had failed to arrange money for her son. My emergency backup money-bank had been robbed, either by my brother or my father. The cab arrived soon after and I took my leave. Just when I was about to step out, I saw tears in her eyes. I had not hugged her, or even cared to say some good words which a mom deserves to hear. But she was a mother. She came up to me and gave me a hug. After a few seconds in her embrace, I said, 'I love you Mom.' It was the voice of my heart, and no planning had gone behind these simple words.

'I plan to visit Nikhil for a month in July. I will be there till 15th August. Do come once, if possible,' she said amidst sobs.

'You know it well enough, Mom. I will not come to his house.'

'You can come to meet me.'

'Ok, I will try…' I said, dismissively.

She gave me the tiffin box she had made for my journey, and I left for Pune, in despair.

I had been on the train for two hours. A hawker came into the compartment, selling biscuits and wafers. I felt like having some, and slipped my hand in the pocket to dig out change. I found a crumpled piece of paper instead.

78

Neel,

I understand the tough time you are going through.

Sorry to say, I asked for money from Nikhil. I did not say anything to you because you might have refused to take Nikhil's help.

The cash is in the tiffin box.

Please do visit your brother.

You might see many shades in a woman, but I see only a son in you.

Your mother.

Twelve

Neel's Mother Talks

I play multiple roles in my life, but that of a mother has been the toughest. As a mother, my job is to take care of the possible and trust god with the impossible. Hi, I am Neel's mother. You might be wondering why I have barged in here.

I know it is Neel's book. He is writing this for a very special reason, and being his mother, I think, I too must say something.

I am certain he will present me to you as a mother, blind to her son's immoralities. The woman who let him continue with his acts, even when she could have made a huge difference. Well, that's because he saw it like that. I was, for him, a mother, who did not have any inkling of the truth of her son's desires. The truth is, I was never blind to anything that happened in front of me or behind my back. I knew quite early on that there was something wrong with Neel; that he was indulging in strange activities only as a repercussion of something else. I want to show you the facet of Neel which even he never noticed himself. But a mother understands what a child never lets on.

When he was born, he had been a cute child with all the makings of a very good-looking man when he would grow up. Don't judge me, for I am a mother, and it is my right to believe my son was the most handsome.

Yet, I was not so naive to ignore that though far better in looks than his brother Nikhil, Neel had too small a heart.

Nikhil, my elder son, was an ideal child. He adored his younger brother. I remember, he used to carry his brother's bag to school till class three. Neel had always been so cute and easy on the eyes. Everyone who visited us played with him and pampered him. He was a favourite doll for all the ladies.

When Neel was in class sixth, I was called to school because he had etched a nude figure on the classroom wooden desk. His class teacher had been livid at his shameful creation. I had known with the first glance that it was Neel's doing. He had always been fascinated with women's legs, I had noticed. I won't deny, the art on that table had been exceptionally good. And I had wondered how he could master all those details of a woman's body. He was, after all, only eleven years old. I had reprimanded him, but he was too young to comprehend such things.

He always asked for unusual gifts. When all boys his age asked for racing cars, roller skates, bicycles, chocolates and ice-creams, he demanded soft toys, Barbie dolls or a doll house, which even girls his age looked down upon. He liked to play with such things.

During his growing up years, I always noticed his curiosity for 'bad' movies, erotic books, adult magazines and other such things. I had noticed, but avoided the issue thinking it was a phase and he would grow out of it. I did not stop him. For me, he was always too young to understand these things.

Once, we were watching the movie *Raja Hindustani*, and the notorious kissing scene between Aamir Khan and Karisma Kapoor came up on the screen. Instinctively, I got up to switch off the TV. In those days, we did not have other channels to flip to. I cursed the Doordarshan people! Why on earth had they not deleted that scene? That day, before falling asleep, Neel had asked, "Are babies born after kissing…?"

He wanted to take Biology in class eleventh, but his father forced him to take maths. He did not resist, but as he grew up, though his looks turned exceptionally good, he grew worse in studies year after year. These changes in his life were completely opposite to that of his brother Nikhil.

Neel chose a couple of friends in his graduation years who smoked and abused drugs. I began finding Neel smelling weird. I asked him a couple of times, casually. He always made senseless excuses. But his wavering eyes and illogical reasons gave away things he was trying hard to hide.

Neel's father also noticed the changes. He stopped Neel's pocket money immediately. He could not see his hard-earned money turning into smoke and delirium.

The bad Neel turned worse. He started stealing things. To some extent, I funded his expenses silently. I wished to avoid anything drastic from happening.

As expected, Nikhil got a job in Satyam as soon as he finished his education, while Neel failed at everything he ever attempted in life. His father refused to even speak to him. Whenever Neel would feel emotional, he would hug me, but he did not cry. It was tough seeing the boy turn into stone, emotionally. I tried to recollect the last time he had cried. It was a shock when I realised it had been way back, when he was in class three. I don't deny we played our parts in it, but eventually my son, who could have been gold, turned into a stone-heart instead.

But Nikhil has a heart of gold. He gave me a small amount of money every month, as a token of respect. Without anyone finding out, I spent it silently on Neel. After all, I am a weak mother too.

Life went on, things remained the same, and the circumstances were manageable. Then suddenly, everything took a turn for the bad, when Nikhil married Neha, a beautiful, talented girl. I noticed Neel eyeing her a couple of times and tried to distract him. I made sure I was around when the two of them interacted, and asked Neel to run some errand if I had to be out. I didn't know what more I could do without disturbing the peace of the house.

One day, he addressed Neha by her name. I had always heard him call her Bhabhi before that. I knew that day, he had broken the sanctity of a beautiful relationship.

I had a premonition where these things were heading, and soon enough, I was proven right. Nikhil mentioned an opportunity to work in TCS Mumbai and I agreed readily.

Neel, on the other hand, had finally fulfilled his dream; of teaching in a school of his choice. He had started working as a mathematics teacher in Pune. When he lost his earlier job, no school in Delhi was willing to accommodate him and he did not hesitate even once before shifting to Pune. My small family broke as both my kids moved out of home. I was devastated.

While Nikhil and Neha settled in quite well in Mumbai, and even Neha started working, Neel began deteriorating further. Out of his father's and brother's watchful gaze, he began showing his objectification for women openly. His comments were sharp and the slangs he used made one cringe. He only thought of women as bodies and their existence, for him, was solely to satisfy men's need. Every time I heard of molestation cases, I would get scared. I prayed to the almighty to give Neel the wisdom to refrain. I knew how he thought, but I could also see that he had conditioned himself in a way that he could camouflage his desires behind sweet talk.

Almost after one year of shifting out, he came from Pune. In a roundabout manner, he asked me for some money. I presumed there was no improvement in his behaviour and must be in trouble owing to that.

I did not have the amount he needed, so I asked Nikhil. I was sure his father was not going to listen to me, even one bit. Nikhil agreed readily to help his younger brother. He immediately transferred thirty thousand rupees to my account, but made a request. He wanted me to make sure that Neel never came to Mumbai. He did not hate him, but did not want to see his face. I was hurt by his condition, and wondered what had led to this? Had he seen him eyeing Neha the way I had? Why would a husband tolerate such a thing? Or had Neha told him something? Whatever that may be, I could only ask when we met. But despite all that, I appreciated his helping his brother. At the core of my heart, I could sense that he still loved his brother. I had not failed as a mother, not completely.

I have continuously tried to pull Neel out of the depths he has fallen into. I call him each Sunday so that he knows someone is keeping a track, someone is watching over, there is someone he can fall back on.

I have tried a lot and failed at many things in life, but I am not one to surrender. I tried to find the reason behind Neel becoming the person that he had. Why he could not think of women in any other way? Was it because he never had a girl so close to him who could change him? Perhaps.

All that said and done, I still believe, one day, my Neel will be a changed man.

Thirteen

I came back to Pune, my pocket warm with mom's financial help, or I should say Nikhil's. I was sure it would tide me over for a while. My full and final job settlement would come after two months. I was relaxed and somewhat happy.

I had barely entered when Pihu came chirping, happy to know I was back, and almost falling over me in her excitement of the same. Annu chided her and ordered her to be back home, and I couldn't thank her enough for it.

That night, I slept comfortably after a long time of restlessness.

Next day, I went to school with an unwanted task at hand. It was the burden of dropping Pihu. My only consolation was that the school would soon close for preparation of exams. I had to survive this duty just for a few days. Moreover, great achievements always start with small sacrifices. Now don't ask me what great achievement! I will just tell you this - I had something great in mind.

After dropping Pihu at the gate and going my way, I found myself to be a victim of weird looks from most teachers and a few students. I could guess what was going on in their mind. How I was with Pihu! It appeared, the entire school was aware of what had happened with me. Rumours are carried by haters, spread by fools and accepted by idiots. So I was the hot topic of the day, the stares said. And walking in with Pihu had only added fuel to the fire, thanks to Pihu's extra bright smile while waving me goodbye.

I just took it in my stride, telling myself it was a matter of a few more days, and went about my work.

▼

Time passes, but some things never change. The school was already closed for preparatory leave. It was Saturday evening and I was tired. Having finished my dinner, I was all set to go to sleep. I decided to double check the lock of the front door, else Pihu walked in, without knocking, like she often did.

But what can stop Pihu? Just as I was settling into my bed, I heard a rap at the door. I knew instantly who it was. It was late in the evening, and I was already frustrated with things going wrong at school. Being seen with Pihu was spoiling my image further. I cursed Pihu in my head and walked to the door.

'Hi sir, how are you?'

Pihu stood there in a pair of pink capris and a loosely fitted purple T-shirt. She was carrying two bulky books in her hand. She looked like she would collapse under the weight of the books and die right there. I took the books from her hands.

'Anything urgent?' I asked coldly.

'Sir, I am weak in maths. Can you teach me?' she said making a puppy face.

It was unbelievable! Had the Ananya episode leaked to the students? Was she mocking me? Or was it just hard luck that whatever happened around me was so weird? I could not leave any scope for Ananya part 2.

'No Pihu,' I stated firmly.

'Why sir? You gave tuitions to Ananya?'

My ears turned hot and red. I could not believe my ears! What did she know about Ananya? I looked at her blankly. Not betraying any emotion, I asked, 'Who said that?'

'She herself did.'

'You know her?'

'We had been classmates. I failed in tenth and Ananya passed.'

The sleepiness had vanished. I wished I could kill myself. It was all so messed up! I stood silently, wondering how best to handle this. Here I was trying to keep this whole episode away from Annu and this house, and this girl Pihu had turned out to be Ananya's friend.

While all these thoughts ran helter skelter in my head, Pihu stood there looking at me with the same innocent face. I gave her the benefit of doubt. Maybe she did not know the entire episode. I heaved a sigh of relief and asked, 'What topics are you facing problems in?' I turned to keep the bulky books on the table.

She beamed, elated that I had somewhat agreed. 'I don't have a specific problem, sir. I request your guidance in entire maths.'

'Maths is a vast topic, Pihu. You need to tell me which part of maths bothers you the most?'

'Algebra,' she said after much deliberation.

'Okay. Why are you so uncomfortable with it?'

'In finalizing the value of x,' she stated victoriously, finally zeroing in on her problem.

Her patent smile irked me the most. I looked around at the bulky, half-a-kilogram of R.S. Aggarwal's *Advanced Maths* books lying on the table. I felt an urge to pick up the books and bang them on her head. Yet again, I controlled my emotions and said, 'X is an unknown number, Pihu. It cannot be valued.'

Fourteen

I promised Pihu I would teach her the next day, as I was tired. She was quite happy that I agreed, and thankfully, left without making any fuss. Now, in bed, trying to sleep, Pihu's words were giving me nightmares! How on earth did she find out about Ananya? Ananya had been behaving like the perfect ego-filled dumb-head, spreading rumours about me. But what else could I expect!

I got up and dug out my whiskey bottle. After downing the third peg, I began feeling the need to be out. The idea of gazing at the river filled my heart with some smiles. It was midnight, so the mother-daughter upstairs would have slept, I was sure.

I prepared myself another large, strong peg and began climbing the stairs in search of fresh air. The terrace was the best thing in this house. Moreover, Pune evenings are awesome. The cool refreshing breeze was slowly caressing my senses, making me feel good. I had a few sips, as I lazily walked from one end to another.

Silence, the sense of peace, allowed me to delve into my inner self. I was transported into thoughts of days to come. The thoughts were not without worries about my past mistakes and the uncertainty of the future. How will I get a job? How long could I hide my truth from Annu? How was I to take care of the unwanted attention from Pihu?

I was occupied with these thoughts when a muffled noise alerted me. It seemed like someone was walking up the stairs. For a second I thought I was hallucinating, but then the source of the disturbance appeared.

In the dim light of the staircase, her features appeared misted, but there was no hiding her slim figure in the grey shorts and sleeveless white t-shirt. Her skin appeared flawless. She was beautiful, I thought, as she stood in front of me.

Annu stood scanning me from top to bottom, as if she had seen an alien. A social suicide! I stood with a coloured liquid in my hand.

For a few seconds, both of us measured each other in silence. Her skimpy shorts and naval length wide necked top said she was not prepared to meet anyone here and the nectar in my hand shouted out that I too had not expected someone to disturb my solitude.

'Hi sir. You here, at this hour? Is everything fine?' she asked politely, her nose crinkling a bit, making her look very cute.

My heart sank momentarily while I nodded. 'Yes, Annu ji,' I murmured, almost hiding my glass. It was as if I was hiding my unofficial girlfriend.

'It's okay, feel free to drink,' Annu said casually, with a wave of her hand.

I nodded in appreciation. She stood undecidedly for a while, then moved to the corner.

She appeared mesmerising. Her slim figure, accentuated by her short dress, could be seen in a new avatar. Many hormones began slipping through my system. After all, being slightly tipsy never helps keep the demon under control.

The calmness of the night, the breathtaking view of the river flowing in the distance, the moon somewhere behind the clouds bathing her with its light, the cool breeze blowing past her to me - it filled the atmosphere with romance.

She stood absolutely silent, staring at the river, as if sending someone silent messages. I could guess she was a regular visitor. She knew exactly where to go and what to do.

I pretended to be Mr Cool, who had nothing to worry about in life. And at the same time, I continued checking her out. Her silence was very disconcerting. It was like a loud cry. Anyone looking at her could make out that something afflicted her deeply. I wanted to ask her the reason for her being so disturbed, but, I guess, it was not the right time.

I finished my drink, and I had been drinking slowly, but she hadn't moved a muscle. I couldn't have said much, so I was all set to move towards the staircase.

'Sir…' I was called. Even in my drunken state, I knew I had heard right. Annu had called me. I turned to face her.

'I needed a small favour, hope you won't say no.'

Can a drunk person say no? If she would have asked for all my wealth, which I anyway didn't have, I would have given it up without a second thought. 'Yes, please.'

'You denied Pihu's request to teach her maths. She is weak in the subject. She already failed class tenth due to maths.' She went quiet, as if thinking back on the tough time.

'She is free to discuss anything at any time,' I said.

'I don't intend to pester, but she wishes to study the entire syllabus from you,' she sounded quite hesitant in putting it out.

'Exams are just around the corner. It's not possible to deal with the entire syllabus,' I said honestly, expecting her to see the sense in my reasoning and come up with some logical answer. But then, the bubble burst, and she behaved in a way expected from Pihu's mom.

I wondered if my reasoning had fallen on deaf ears when she said, 'Actually… you are her favourite teacher.'

I wanted to ask why! I had never taught her before, or met her. 'Okay, the whole syllabus?' I asked resignedly.

Annu nodded.

I was reluctant. This would give Pihu a free pass to tag on to me, at all times. I didn't wish to get into another controversy. I might have been in a half unconscious state, yet I made a clear point, 'No problem! But I will teach her in your house, not in my portion. I hope you understand.'

Her smile reappeared magically, and I gave myself a pat on the back. After all, it was my double stroke. First, I would create a good impression, and second, I would get to be around Annu.

'Can I ask you one thing?' I decided to use this opportunity to find answers of questions that had been troubling me.

'Yes please,' she looked at me squarely.

'Only two members… in a two-storey house? I am sorry, but are there more? And this house belongs to you? I mean, isn't it too much for two people?'

Her smile was now a faint one. 'Actually, this house had belonged to my husband. After his demise, I got everything that was in his name. So, I am the owner of the house.'

Why had a modern, independent widow not remarried? The question began its rounds in my already fuzzy head, but we were not close enough for me to ask her that.

'What would be the fee, sir?'

I made some mental calculations, but to no avail. No matter how much I had soaked, I always fell short of money. So technically, nothing would be enough. This time, I decided to make a long-term investment, and hit the nail on its head.

'I cannot charge anything. After all, Pihu is my favourite student.'

▼

Aarav and I were in the cafeteria the next day, waiting for the tea to be served. The staff had to be there for doubt clearing sessions, even during preparatory leave. I was not much of a talker, but I was missing those heart to heart chats with my only friend Aarav. When in staff accommodation, it was so simple to catch up.

That's when someone neither a beauty nor with brain, passed by the teachers' café.

I had a bad feeling. There was no limit to Pihu's immaturity.

She waved at me and looked like she wanted to say something. Though I offered an unwilling smile, I pretended as if she was talking to someone sitting on Mars or Jupiter. Aarav gave me a strange look.

'Hi!' My lips moved as I waved back at her, of course with a plastic smile.

'Why are you behaving like this?' Aarav asked.

'Nothing yaar. This girl has made my life hell,' I spoke, the smile still plastered to my face.

'Congratulations on the new girlfriend!' He said with a sly look.

'She is not my girlfriend!" I glared at him, taking offense. 'Are you out of your mind?'

'But the way she is waving at you, offered her house almost for free, speaks clearly of her intentions.'

'That is the problem.'

'Let me give you the rumour.'

'Rumour?' Not again, I thought.

'Everyone knows you have two girlfriends.'

'What nonsense! Really?'

Aarav nodded, taking pleasure in my displeasure.

'And how does *everyone* know them?'

'You are famous after Ananya's case.'

'This is so frustrating! Who is spreading these false reports? And how on earth did people get to know about Pihu?'

'You come to school with her,' he said as if it was the most obvious explanation. 'And second, Ananya is notorious.'

I took a deep breath. Suddenly things had become too weird. 'What is the rumour?'

'The famous hunk of a teacher, who likes teenagers.'

I groaned. Seriously! Why were all these fucking things happening to me?

'This girl will spoil my plan,' I mumbled shaking my head.

'What plan?'

'Remember, I told you about Pihu's mom…'

'The widow?' he said dismissively.

95

'Don't speak of her in that tone… I like her,' I said softly.

'You like her?' he frowned. He pulled out the middle finger and acted as if he was gagging, because I had puked some shit which he was finding hard to swallow.

'She is the owner of an independent house.'

'So, you are planning to indulge with your girlfriend's mom, just because she owns an expensive house?'

'Stop calling her my girlfriend!' I snapped at Aarav.

'Okay sorry.' He raised his hands in surrender and added, 'But it is a bad deal.'

'Why?'

'They will find out about Ananya and you.'

'That is my only worry. Pihu knows something about Ananya. She was questioning me about it. What if she tells the same to her mom?'

'That is a genuine problem… but, I have a solution for you.'

This was Aarav, my friend. He always resisted and tried to hold me back, but ended up supporting me by coming up with his stupid ideas. I nodded. Though I had never taken Aarav's suggestions seriously earlier, his confidence this time was making me confident too.

'You can use Pihu's love to climb the ladder to her mom.'

Fifteen

That day, I took time to dress up. I reached for my crisp white and blue checked shirt and the dark brown chinos that had been sitting in the cupboards' upper shelf, waiting for a good occasion. Making sure my hair was neat, I applied a generous coating of petroleum jelly to add that extra softness to my lips. I even sprayed the perfume a lady friend had gifted. My freshly shaven face was radiant, as I folded the clean white handkerchief and slipped it in the back pocket. I was all set to meet Pihu for my first scheduled tuition class, and the reason I was spending time in front of the mirror was, of course, Annu.

I knocked, expecting Annu to appear in one of her sexily smart dresses, but the door opened and Pihu gave me a half hug. She behaved as if I was one of her old pals. Automatically, my face turned stiff with irritation. It was beyond me, the reason why she was always more than just happy to see me.

Pihu wore short pants, too short for her! I could see her thin, unwaxed legs, and the loose T-shirt hung on her like a big fat dress resting on a slim hanger.

I diverted my attention from her legs to my surroundings.

'Sir, it's good to see you!' My line of thoughts was interrupted by Annu. She welcomed me with a sugar sweet smile as she came out to greet me.

I really liked Annu. But it was for more than just her looks. Of course, I could not entirely disregard her beauty, but she was well-mannered, seemed mature, and single-handedly managed everything.

The lounge had an old four-seater sofa. It was quite outdated, but new covers hid its age well. Behind it was an old and faded wooden dining table, next to the modular kitchen.

The layout of the ground floor and the first floor was slightly different, as rooms were placed after the kitchen.

Annu guided me to an inner room. The walls were lined with pictures, but I couldn't have a good look at them. There were some childish drawings. I guessed, Pihu would have made them during her growing years, and the doting mother had held on to them.

The room which I entered had a study table and two chairs placed at right angles, clearly the designated place for me to teach. The room was meticulously clean. Either they were too organized, or it had been cleaned and arranged to make space for me.

I sat on one of the chairs, and sneakily studied the room. My eyes fell on the right side of the wardrobe; the corner appeared like a hospital's chamber. There was a drip rod, some bottles, a few syringes, clean white towels, sanitizer bottle, several medicines, and bundles of bigger-sized diapers. I concluded Annu practised nursing from her home as well. Couldn't blame her, she had to manage her finances.

A picture, this one a family photo, hung at the centre of the wall. A young couple was holding a baby. The frame was almost three meters away from me, but I could recognize the young girl in the picture. She was glowing, looked extremely happy, and the brightness of her eyes captured me. I could not stop myself from thinking how beautiful she was. The same lady came into the room with a glass of water. I looked at her, and my mind said – she is still just as beautiful.

'Thanks,' I picked the glass of water.

She nodded and turned her face slightly away to scream, 'Pihuuuu… where are you? Come here, sir is waiting…'

'Just two minutes, Mumma…' Pihu answered from some corner of the house.

'Neel sir, what would you like to have… tea or coffee?'

I liked tea. Hoping to make a civilized impression, I said, 'Coffee, without milk.'

She smiled brightly, which was enough to please a pervert like me.

She left the room. Inadvertently, my eyes travelled back to the family photo. I couldn't stop looking at it. I guessed the baby in the image to be Pihu. The Pihu in the photo was a chubby and healthy child. Unwillingly, but out of curiosity, my eyes moved on to the man in the picture. I focussed on him. I had a feeling I knew him. He looked familiar. I was sure I had seen this man before. I tried to shuffle through the images of people I had met and tried to think hard, but could not place this man.

'Hi, sir!' Pihu had finally decided to come to the room. She seemed excited, 'Which chapter shall we start with?'

'Algebra… Isn't that the part which troubles you the most?'

My nostrils were tickled by the wafting aroma of the coffee that Annu placed in front of me. I rolled up the sleeves of my shirt and held the coffee mug, James Bond style. Pihu sat across from me, blushing for no apparent reason. She did not look interested in the book at all.

'The problems won't solve themselves if you keep looking at me. Focus!' I chided.

'Nice shirt, sir. You look cool in it.'

I had worn this shirt for her mom and this teenager was noticing it? I didn't know what to say to her. And it didn't help that she was blushing like I was about to propose to her.

'Pihu, if you stop looking at me, we can get back to work.'

'No sir, I am angry with you,' she faked a let-down-face.

Was I here to please my angry girlfriend? 'What did I do to get you angry?' I took the coffee mug to my lips.

'You like mom more than me,' Pihu stated matter-of-factly.

I coughed as the scalding coffee burnt the back of my throat. I had had too much in one gulp and the almost bitter taste burnt me down. Add to that her words which led to all this chaos in the first place. It felt like, I was about to get a heart attack! 'And what makes you say that?' I counter questioned, to confirm if my liking was all that evident.

'Because when I asked for your help in maths, you denied. And then you agreed to mom's request,' Pihu explained.

I heaved a sigh of relief. 'Oh that!'

She nodded and I looked at her book. 'Can we please focus on studies?' I raised my voice a little. In a few minutes, I concluded her algebra was at an unsalvageable stage. I decided to focus on weak sections instead, rather than pursuing all topics. I thought I'd let her say which was the weakest section – quadratic equations, trigonometry or whatever.

I pointed at the contents page listing all these options and asked her, 'So Pihu, which is the hardest subject for you?'

'I don't like politics,' Pihu shook her head for effect.

'I am not asking your topics of interest. I meant the toughest unit in maths!' Suddenly, teaching felt like the toughest job. If I spent any more time with Pihu, I was sure to start hating my job.

She remained silent.

'In which part of this section can you not solve any problems at all?' I poked again, simplifying the question for her, and pointing at the sections listed in contents once again.

'Probability...'

'Okay. You only need to concentrate; it's not that difficult.' I picked the book and flipped the pages.

'Sir, can I ask a question?'

I nodded, still looking at the book.

'Was Ananya good in studies?'

It was impossible to handle this girl. She had no mood to study, and I wondered why she was snooping. Where was she getting to know about these things?

'Can we focus on this chapter, Pihu?' I repeated with a tough face. I had realized by now that being polite would not work with Pihu. I began explaining with an example, 'Suppose, Pihu, there are two students and one teacher. The teacher has four hours to teach, and the students are sitting at two different places. What chance does each student get to study?'

'Two hours,' Pihu answered.

'Correct. What percent is two of four?'

'Fifty percent.'

'Right! So what would be the probability for a student to get the teacher's time?'

'Probability would be 50%,' she said with a winner's smile.

I smiled back in appreciation and said, 'Very good!'

'But I have a doubt, sir,' she said.

'Hope it's related to what we are studying?'

'Of course, sir!' she said in a tone implying she never asked any other kind. 'Suppose one student is Pihu, and the second is Ananya. And you love to spend time with only one. In that case, what would be the probability of the other student getting to spend time with you?'

This was unbelievable! I seethed, wishing I could run off, or maybe bang the notebook on her head. I looked at her disbelievingly. She was smiling, as if she had cracked the biggest joke.

I answered with clenched teeth, 'Zero probability for you to learn mathematics.'

Sixteen

Weed or Marijuana makes you feel silly, relaxed, sleepy, happy, even nervous and scared. Though illegal in India, it is readily available. The only rule to follow while having awesome weed is - it cannot be consumed without pals.

Everything that had happened in the recent past was too much on my nerves and I definitely needed to be high. I purchased a bundle and called my partner in crime.

'Hey, Aarav! How are you buddy?'

'Hey Neel. I was missing you since morning!'

'Woah! Missing me? Why use these girly words, man? All well?'

'Everything is fine now. Let's meet!' Aarav suggested cheerfully, and I readily agreed.

Aarav had always been the one to agree to my plans. And his having taken initiative pleasantly surprised me.

Since Aarav had always been around, I had never felt bored. I was so used to him, I never noticed his presence. Little did I know that this day was to teach me an important lesson - Never undermine the presence of a friend who has always been there for you.

In a few minutes, I picked Aarav from outside the school hostel. We had decided to go to Lonavla for a break. We had been there on many occasions before, and it was our favourite adda outside the city.

My Pulsar was heading at a speed of sixty km/h as we entered the highway. The expressway had proved its mettle. You could reach from Pune to Mumbai in just two hours, and Lonavala was just under an hour away by bike. The view of the valley below, from the expressway, was a picture out of a child's scrapbook. The vehicles down below looked like tiny Lego blocks, and you could spend a lifetime on the roadside with the floating clouds covering the plateaus, the numerous frothy waterfalls – big and small- flowing with temperamental might. There was lush greenery all around, and from experience, we knew monsoon was the best season to be in this place. Though we were a little early, it was still pretty breathtaking.

The usually jubilant Aarav was silent today. I had assumed from the chirpiness in his voice a while ago that he'd be excited, but now, I couldn't make out if he was okay. On earlier occasions, he used to sing horny cheap songs while we rode along, which only boys drenched in lust could sing.

'What happened, Aarav? Are you alright?' I finally asked.

'Yes,' Aarav answered.

'Why are you so quiet then?' I tried to look over my shoulder while driving the bike.

'Today is my birthday,' he said slowly.

'Really?' I slowed the bike and hollered, 'Happy birthday, dude!'

'Thanks!' he whispered back.

This was not expected on his birthday! There must have been something on his mind, but, as usual, lost in my own life, I ignored his silence. I told you, I was bad at keeping relationships.

We continued the drive and reached the Bhushi dam. We had come here first during monsoons, and had been mesmerized at the overflowing water. It was a beautiful sight. But when it came to a rendezvous of two notorious friends, they had to discover new places, where no one else could find them. We also had. Behind the dam, there were a few sites, quite unexplored. We had been to those spots before. There was a beautiful view of the lake from one particular spot, which we both loved. We reached that spot after walking for some twenty minutes. I studied the surrounding from my position. Once assured no one was watching us, I extracted the pouch from under my shirt.

'Aarav, come on! Show me your expertise in making these joints, man!' I had a smile on my face, as if we were going to make a big achievement in the moments to follow.

He nodded, stretching his hand out.

I opened the packed weed and he got a glimpse.

'OMG! How did you manage to get that much of it? Are they selling it on discount?' Aarav was astonished to see the prosperity of a teacher, who was not even salaried anymore.

'It will go a long way, bro! We will use only a little.'

I pulled out a small quantity of the herb while Aarav removed the tobacco from the cigarette. I filled the cigarette with our favourite, all set to become one with the heavens above.

I lit Aarav's joint and then mine. We took a deep drag each, both silent. Once comfortable with the changes it was bringing, a fire began to burn within me. It seemed my loneliness had caught up with me. Not having been able to talk to anyone in so many days, I couldn't bring myself to stop now. I had met Aarav also only in school and thought there was much I needed to tell him. So I started off. And I spoke about everything that came into my head – from my loneliness, to my bankruptcy; from how many girls I had slept with to my liking for Annu. I didn't stop even to breathe when I spoke about how I had started liking Annu, and how my hatred for Pihu was rising consistently.

Aarav was painstakingly silent. If he wasn't sitting there in front, I wouldn't know of his presence. Usually, Aarav could never remain quiet after a few puffs. It was something impossible to picture. Yet, here he sat, quietly and intently looking at me. Either my money was wasted on ineffective weed, or there was something bothering him.

When we own our mind, we talk sense; when something else owns it, we talk about useless things. So I started talking about money.

I pulled out my purse. 'Hey, here is your ten thousand. All accounts settled. Thanks for your help.' I smiled handing him five crisp two thousand-rupee notes. I still had several of those pink beauties in my wallet.

'Where did you get all that money from? You've already resigned. You could not have got the salary or the full and final settlement from school?' Aarav asked curious.

I laughed! A fool's laugh, for no reason.

'I am a rich man, bro! I have mom and mom has her obedient son, who always funds my expenses. My emotional brother!' I said with disdain. The weed was doing its job well.

'Someone helps you, and you make fun of them?' Aarav looked at me, disapproving.

'What can I say? My brother is an emotional man,' I repeated, least bothered about what he was getting at.

'I also help you,' Aarav said moodily.

'Yaar, you are my bro.' I patted my pal on the back, happy to be with him.

'What kind of bro am I?'

He was hell bent on busting my high. I could not understand why he had started this stupid conversation.

'Boss, do not spoil my joint! I paid one thousand for that.'

'At least you care for this joint!' he said and looked away.

My state of high suddenly vanished. Something was bothering him, giving him a hard time. I did not poke him. Instead, I stared at the lake. There was silence. In the distance, a few couples jumped into the water. People let out shrieks of delight as they danced in water flowing from the dam. Only the two of us were missing out on all the fun.

I thought of changing the mood a bit, and finally spoke, 'Bro, don't spoil your mood. It's your birthday today!'

The look on his face suddenly changed as he looked up at me with almost bloodshot eyes. 'You are damned right, Neel! Today is my birthday.' There was sarcastic sneer on his face as he said, '...and for the past hour, we are talking about Pihu, and her mom... and... and how many girls you freaking fucked! Or maybe how you fooled your mother for money...' he kicked a pebble with too much unnecessary force, '...Haven't we been discussing my birthday for the past hour or so?'

His outburst stunned me. I threw away the joint.

'Sorry yaar! I… my emotions don't work…'

Aarav cut me short, 'Today is my birthday, Neel. I had been missing my family since morning, and then I thought, I have a friend to celebrate with. When you called, I thought it was for my birthday. But you freaking didn't even know that!'

'Sorry yaar. You are my best buddy…'

'No, I think I am just your time-pass. You call me only when you get bored.'

He was fuming, and I didn't know if anything I said would make things better or worse. So I kept quiet. Hoping to give him a chance to say all the things which he had been keeping within him for so long.

'Tell me something, Neel! What are you? You are not a good son, not a good brother, and today, I am certain, you are not even a good friend.'

Seventeen

Aarav Speaks

Hello there! I am Aarav. The same guy who Neel says is his only friend. How I wish he would have said 'his best friend'.

When Neel came to me with the peculiar request to write something about him, I denied. A clear no it was. He emphasised that he wanted to write a true story. That was when I decided to write for him. After all, I am his only friend.

I teach English in DAV school, and worked with Neel for a while. I had been at the school for three years when Neel joined as the maths teacher.

The first thing that made me pay attention to him was his looks. I might sound cheesy, but that's how it was! Since I am not what you normally call good-looking, Neel's exceptionally charismatic looks were an eye-catcher. His fair complexion, sparkling dark brown eyes, soft yet masculine full lips, the brownish smooth hair, his square shoulders, the long legs, lean muscled arms, give him a seductive personality. You get to see manly specimen of beauty like him only in erotic movies.

We had a couple of interactions as colleagues, but our friendship progressed beyond a certain level when we exchanged downloaded movies.

'Do you have any adult quality stuff?' I had asked.

He counter-questioned, 'What is your type?'

Type! Never had I given it that much thought. Could there be so many variations?

Reading the ignorance written on my face, Neel rattled off the classifications, 'Amateur, oral, big breasts, threesomes, anal, gay... You don't have to be a sex-expert to know there is porn for pretty much any taste.' Neel pursed his full lips and shrugged casually.

This was new! Was I so behind my generation, I wondered? I acted smart. 'I think amateur would be my type,' I said the first word I remembered from his list.

Neel looked at me blankly, 'What in amateur?'

I did not react, and he vomited a list again. 'I mean, what is your taste? Monster porn, play acting, cat costume porn...'

I lost my interest in porn right there and then. Sex delayed is sex denied.

His laptop's D-Drive was full of those lists, and the dry sponge that I was in this area, I sucked up the information greedily. And since bad habits always gave good friends, we started sharing thoughts on everything. He had amazing skills of narrating a story. We started discussing girls. Let me confess, as I have committed to only writing the truth, I too was interested in girls. And why not!

We shared experiences and fantasies with each other, for the lack of any of us having a girlfriend. Sometime on, I realized that Neel was a pervert. My liking for girls emanated from a deep human desire, his was all that he thought about. Plus, he liked teens. I do not know why? Wonder what in them fanaticizes him?

He always talked about beautiful girls. I have lost count of the evenings we have spent in Phoenix mall just to watch naked legs. We've spent hours watching girls in skirts and shorts. But, we never crossed our boundaries. That was always an unsaid rule.

When he started indulging Ananya, I raised my concern. Even warned him. That girl has ruined a whole lot of boys in her batch, and Neel is a self-confessed slave to his body. As he went deeper into the stint with Ananya, I figured, he was killing his own future.

My fear for my friend turned into reality soon after. He realised his mistake of leading her on, and stopped her from coming to his place, but it was too late. Someone complained about his relationship with Ananya. He was asked to leave the campus. And then Pihu landed out of the blue. To this date, I cannot make out why that girl supported him and asked him to move into her house.

I had taught Pihu English in class tenth. She was an irregular student and I remember clearly because I had even complained to her mother, who had given some medical excuse.

I surmised Pihu was another Neel. What kind of a girl would have a crush on her teacher who was eleven years older to her?

In a bid to know more and ensure that Neel wasn't landing himself into more trouble, I launched into an investigation about her. Pihu's father had passed away around five years back, but I could not discover the cause of his death. When I found out about her loss, for the first time I felt some sympathy for Pihu.

What made my sympathy vanish was the way Pihu looked at Neel and tried to dominate over him. It was not right! I mean, a girl her age could get easily infatuated, and Neel had to put his foot down. But then again, the inevitable happened and my friend Neel applied his brain. He started going after Pihu's mother. What a complex situation! Student fishing her teacher and the teacher looking to lure the student's mother.

Anyway, it was when he lost the job and any hope of immediate financial help that he showed me a fat gold chain that he had purloined from his sister-in-law some time ago. He had done it to have a backup in case of emergency for money. He asked me a few thousand rupees in exchange for that chain. From the circumstances he described, I realised, he had brutally murdered a pure relationship. That was the first time I disliked him. He had cheated on his own brother! A brother who had always helped him.

I concluded thereafter that Neel was actually a bad man. He never cared for anyone. I always thought I was his valued friend, but he was far from such emotions. He was surely a person without emotions, just a human figure crafted out of stone.

You might wonder if I had realised he was so bad, then why am I still his friend? That's because I know, he may be bad and emotionless, but he had a few good bones in his body too. He never forced anyone for intimacy. He always prayed for other people. He was far from jealously and hatred. He could be bad in one case, but still, there was some humanity left in him. I know, he always tried to help everyone, but he could not express his emotions.

I am certain, life will teach him a lesson, and I pray for it to happen soon. He was not a good man, not a good brother, a good son, and yes, I regret to say, not a good friend too.

But I am sure, one day, he will change. I have seen a good heart in a bad soul.

Eighteen

As school closed down for exams, I lost my sole means of livelihood, and time-pass. I was always in the house, either reading novels or looking for jobs. I had not yet been called for any interview. All the schools were closed for the next few months and the new session would start only in July. March to June is anyway the dry season for teachers' hiring.

Too much time in hand and the absence of a good friend is the most unpleasant combination to be living with. I was in my room, looking for things to do. My eyes fell on the full-size mirror. I noticed, the person in the mirror was not happy. Somewhere in my heart, I had a bad feeling about myself. I tore my eyes away from the mirror, reaching for the whisky bottle. I made a large peg, and finished it in one go. I did not want to be that unhappy man. I wanted to forget that feeling, to lose my senses. I downed two large pegs, played a song on my phone, and slept peacefully.

The next day, I made a call long overdue. To Aarav, my friend. I am not sure I felt all that emotionally or not, but I surely could not afford to lose him. He was upset because of the fiasco on his birthday and I was surely to blame. So I called him up and apologized. He waved it off with his words, saying he had lost temper because he was missing his family. But I knew he was disappointed. But what could an emotionally barren man like me do!

Days were unending, but evenings were the most difficult to pass. While people waited eagerly for the evening, so that they could go out to have fun with friends or spend some time with family, I dreaded it. There was no work to keep me.

I finally picked my lazy bones up and stepped into the overgrown garden. Outside the gate, there was silence on the road. I had noticed that in this colony, kids played in assigned areas, carefully, without making any excess noise.

I was so lonely, I started longing for Pihu's company, actually. She would have come and disturbed me a million times till now, but I wondered where she was.

My wait ended when I found Pihu leaning on the balcony a few minutes later. I waved at her, smiling broadly. I was afraid my smile could be interpreted wrongly. Pihu waved back eagerly. She took a seat on the plastic chair with her patent smile, gazing at me.

I had never seen her go out with friends or to play. In spite of being weak in studies, she did not even go outside for tuitions. I voiced my thoughts aloud, 'Why don't you go outside and play with your friends?'

'I am not allowed to play with them,' Pihu said emotionlessly.
'Why?'

'Mom doesn't allow me to go outside,' she made a face this time.

I nodded slowly, considering her words. Pihu hardly ever listened to her mom. What little interaction I had with Annu, she did not seem like an authoritarian.

'Will you play with me, sir?' Pihu asked.

I did not know how to react, but I found myself nodding. 'What game would you want to play?'

'Thank you, sir,' Pihu squealed. 'I am coming.'

She took some time in coming down. She was meticulously slow, taking seconds to climb down two steps. It was hard to believe she was seventeen years old! I thought of the possible games both of us could play. I was not in a mood to make mud houses or card palaces. Pihu came near me with a board and a box and sat on the ground.

'Can we play this?'

'What is this?'

'Ludo, my favourite!'

▼

Last time, I had seen Annu on the terrace on Saturday night. I was hoping to get lucky again. It would be the only opportunity to talk to my beauty with brain. I began going to the terrace almost every night. I wanted to present it as a habit, you know. That way, she would not consider my presence fishy. I would carry along my whiskey sometimes; it was my companion when I wanted to be alone. And even if not Annu, the Mula river rejuvenated me quite a bit.

Finally, like all my plans till date, this one was also a success. Almost around midnight on Saturday, a gorgeous single mom in shorts and t-shirt walked up the stairs to the terrace. It was difficult to believe she had a daughter almost seventeen years old. Her skin defied any rules of age, and she glowed in the dim light. Moreover, how could she dress in something so modern! We see widows in white sarees, howling themselves to death, and singing those heart-wrenching songs, which could melt even Hitler's heart.

'Hi, sir,' she said ever so softly.

'Hi,' was all I could say.

'You come here every day?'

'Almost. Mostly when I have trouble sleeping.'

'You have a sleeping problem?'

'Not really. It's more like, I love the beautiful view and it feels good to spend time here.'

'Valid point.' She smiled in appreciation and went to the same corner to convey her ritual message. Her short hair waved in the cool, refreshing breeze from the river. Her eyes had widened, trying to catch a greater view. I could assess all this because I was facing in the same direction, though from a different corner. How I wished terraces had just one corner.

I tried to give an impression that I had no interest in her presence. I began walking the length of the terrace, more to grab her attention than anything else. But Annu was silent, looking content with her life. She seemed to be fully engrossed in her conversation with the river. But all that said, I was sure she carried something in her heart. Although I did not have any emotional bonding with her, still her presence was giving me weird butterflies in the stomach. She stood there silently for nearly half an hour. I got bored to death. I could not even see

AJAY K PANDEY

her properly, it was a dark night. Once done with talking to the
river, she turned and asked, 'So, you are not drinking today?' She
looked at me the same way Pihu did.

'I am not a regular drinker... just rarely.'

'Rare…? Once in a week?' She smiled. She had a good sense
of humour.

I had no worries about the topic of conversation. I was only
happy that we had managed to break the ice. 'You hate people
who drink?'

'No. Even I drink when I am upset.'

I smiled and spoke in my mind, *so today you are not upset*.

'A small request ma'am…'

'Don't call me ma'am.'

'Great. So, you can stop calling me sir. Call me Neel.'

She smiled, 'You are right, Mr Neel.'

We had some conversation regarding Pihu. We discussed
good places to eat and several other mundane things. I had a
feeling she was opening up to me. I decided to ask the important
question which had been revolving in my mind for such a long
time now.

'Annu, could I ask you something personal? I hope you won't
get offended.'

She said, 'Yes, please.'

'What happened to your husband?'

'He passed away due to a genetic disorder,' she said in a
reflex action.

There were no emotions in her words. No hesitation. No
regrets. She must have answered that question hundreds of
times. If the same sentence had come up in a Karan Johar movie,

it might have given you four songs and a gallon of tears for free! She was sad, I could see. I had surely spoiled her mood. There was silence as we both stared at the Mula river.

'Neel, can I ask you a personal question?'

I was on cloud hundred! I heard melodious chirping of imaginary birds, pleasant gush of waves. I was dancing internally, wild in hope that she was getting personal with me.

'Yes please…'

'Did you really love Ananya?'

Suddenly, all those butterflies in my stomach had a cardiac arrest. It was like she had snapped me into two pieces and threw me back into reality. I regretted ever having met Ananya!

'No, Annu. She was just a student.'

'Then why were you asked to leave the school?'

I felt a blankness engulfing me. I regretted coming to the terrace to break the ice with her. The ice had broken on my head! I didn't have anything to say. There was no explanation of what went wrong. And what could I tell her now? If I had come clean earlier on, it would have given me some credibility. I was so shocked that she knew!

I asked her the only question that mattered the most to me, 'How do you know about these school matters?'

She shifted her gaze away from the river to look straight into my eyes, 'My husband was a teacher in your school.'

Nineteen

*id you really love Ananya? Why were you asked to leave
the school…?*

The questions Annu had asked haunted me long after I had
turned around and come back to my room. Sleep was far away. I
tried to make sense of what she had asked.

She knew everything about me! I couldn't stop wondering
why she had allowed me to stay in this house then? Knowing full
well about the scandal - that I had been accused of indulging
with a student! Why charge me negligible rent? Why this favour?
Why does she look at me as if she has known me for ages? Why
does Pihu behave like that with me? Why is Pihu not allowed to
play outside?

Questions, strange questions, floated around my head.
There was something beyond my understanding. The mother
and daughter were keeping some secret close to their hearts.
When and how will this mystery unravel, I was not sure. I had
failed to relate something very important.

I was sitting with Aarav in the school cafeteria the next day.
There was absolute silence around. Tough to believe that it was

the same place which buzzed with students' chorus at all times. I had never seen my work place like that before. Well, it no longer was my place of work anyway.

'Why do you look so tense, Neel?'

'Everything is weird, Aarav. Initially I had thought Pihu is immature. Now I feel, she… they… are strange. The entire family is mad.'

'What happened?'

'They know the rumours around Ananya. Why I was sacked from school… everything! Apparently Pihu's father used to teach here before he passed away.' Aarav's expression changed a bit. 'I fail to understand why they allowed me to stay in their house… nearly without rent, despite knowing everything?'

'Maybe because Pihu loves you,' Aarav offered sarcastically.

'Good, at least one of us finds it funny.' I took an irritated deep breath, 'I am jobless, and can be thrown out of that house anytime… and you are coming up with jokes here!'

'Cool down Neel! I have information for you.' Now he was back with his mojo!

I stared at Aarav expectantly. Aarav said, as if giving out world's darkest secret, 'Ananya's parents did not complain against you.'

'Then who did?'

'Some student… It was a hand-written note. Ananya herself could have, I don't know.'

'It hardly matters now.' I shook my head, 'Tch… I am worried, how did Annu find out.'

'She may know some teachers, you know.'

Suddenly something clicked. I could probably find answer to things that were bugging me. 'I need a small favour.'

'Anything, just don't ask me to request them to tear off your resignation.'

'No, man! Listen, I cannot access office information, but you can! Annu's husband was a teacher in this school. I want to see who Annu's husband was.'

'Why? How is that going to help?'

'I don't know,' I said, confused. 'I am just curious maybe.'

'Hmm, okay! What was his name?'

'Mangesh Parkhi.' I had seen the name on Pihu's school identity card.

Aarav got to his feet. 'I have to leave now. Will let you know what I find.'

I nodded.

Once back home, a new set of questions juggled in my head. Who could have complained about me and Ananya? I recognised her handwriting. Could I see the note? Or a picture of it maybe? More importantly, how was I going to find a job again?

There was a knock at the door. I was sure it was another trouble knocking. I anticipated a second louder knock, but it was soft. There was silence, and after about ten seconds, someone knocked uncertainly. It wasn't Pihu, clearly.

I shook my head, allowing my hair to attain its customary fall. I glanced at the bed and around the room, ascertaining nothing nasty was lying around. I opened the door with an excitement, 'Hi Annu! Pleasure to see you.'

'Hi, sorry to disturb you at this time...'

'No, no, it's perfectly fine. Come in!' I was uncomfortable inviting a beautiful lady to my bachelor pad.

'No, I will take only a minute of your time. I do not wish to intrude, but I know you are looking for a job. I have contacts in some coaching institutes. Competitive exams are coming up in the next two months, and they have requirement for maths faculty. In case you wish to teach, I could refer you.'

A job offer! She wants me to be around. Was it a reason for me to worry?

'If you could, I shall be obliged.'

'Would it be possible for you to share your CV?'

'I will, thanks.'

She smiled, her glossy lips holding my gaze.

'I wonder how you know someone in a coaching centre?' I knew Pihu did not go to any.

'Actually, my husband used to teach there,' Annu replied.

'Oh…' I said uncertainly, 'I am sure… this would be great help. What did Mr Mangesh teach?'

123

'Maths and physics.' She smiled as she left, while I stood there with fresh questions rolling across my head. If Mangesh taught the subject, how come Pihu was a disaster in it? And why was Pihu not sent to any coaching institute? Wasn't Annu concerned about her future?

Twenty

I took almost twenty minutes to get ready. Pulling on a crisply ironed white shirt, I applied my favourite perfume, which many women had told me was quite seductive, and strapped on the first copy of Prado. The most lavish status symbol on a man's body is a watch, and the irony is, no one uses it to tell the time.

It was tutoring time! I was all set to impart knowledge to the poor girl. I had to bear her for at least an hour. I entered her bedroom cum Annu's medical room. While walking inside, I caught a glimpse of Annu, engrossed in her laptop in the other room.

I assigned a few questions to Pihu to work on and began analysing the place. The picture on the wall again became my focus. I urged my brain to tell me about the man in the picture. I was sure I knew him from somewhere; it was just so hard to recollect. I stared into his eyes, waiting for some memory to click, but failed.

'Sir, I have a question,' Pihu called for my attention, reminding me I was here on a job. The toughest job for a man – to teach Pihu.

'Hope it's related to maths.'

She gave a weird childish smile.

'How was Ananya in maths?'

I glared at her, more like a monster. I wished I could bang the entire universe over her. But her innocent looking face and presence of her mom in the house forced me to keep a check on my emotions and act polite.

'I have no idea.'

'Weren't you teaching her maths?' There was a noticeable change in her demeanour.

'Is it so important... that you cannot focus on your studies?' I was barely holding on to my rage.

'No, that's not so important. What I want to say is... she is a bad girl.' Pihu finished with tight lips, as if passing a judgement.

'And how do you know that, Pihu?' I asked exasperatedly.

'She herself told me...'

I looked at her wide-eyed, not knowing what to expect.

'...that she was going to your place for tuitions,' she finished.

I held my head, going blank for minutes.

'Sir, I am fed up of studies!' she declared.

What a coincidence! Even I was fed up of teaching her. It was impossible to teach a student who refused to put in the barest of effort to learn.

'In that case, I think I will leave.' I checked my watch. Still fifteen minutes short of an hour. I would have to sit here for fifteen more minutes, at least. 'Anything else you want to ask? We still have some time...' I glared meaningfully, '...only related to studies.'

'That's great!' She exclaimed gleefully and demanded, 'I want you to tell me a story.'

'Story? What are you talking about?' It was unbelievable.

'I am bored of listening to the same story from my mom. I am sure you would know better stories.'

'Your mother tells you stories?' I tried to look shocked, though I knew about it.

'Yes. Every night. I do not sleep unless my mom narrates a story... it's my favourite part of the day.'

My respect for Annu grew multiple times. How could she bear with this girl every day? I took a steadying breath. My mouth twisted into a sarcastic smile as I asked, 'What kind of story do you want to hear?'

Her answer was unexpected for a seventeen-year-old. 'Why don't you tell me a love story... of an angel and a demon?'

I replied thoughtfully, 'There can be no love between an angel and a demon.'

Twenty-one

I wanted to talk to Ananya. I did not miss her or anything, just that certain things had to be closed. Officially.

I asked Aarav to convey my message to Ananya. I wanted to meet her outside the campus. Not in a public place; it was too risky to be spotted with her. But not in a closed space too; I did not trust her anymore. After much deliberation, Aarav suggested we meet at Ozone, Pune's famous food joint located not far from the school.

She had a Scooty, so reaching the place was not a problem for her. When she came, her face was covered like a dacoit – you couldn't see anything other than her eyes. This appearance was a popular summer delight in Pune, though. It helped Pune girls protect themselves from tanning and at the same time hide their identity.

From my seat, I watched her as she unwrapped the scarf, slowly revealing her face. Taking a look around the room, she walked towards me, her long legs clad in dark blue jeans and the soft yellow t-shirt clinging to her taut chest.

'How are you, sir? Where are you these days?' She hugged me as she asked.

I did not reply. In fact, I was fuming with anger. She was still wandering in her juvenile carelessness. In spite of her smart dress, she did not look attractive to me. I looked at her eyes. I had only hatred for her in mine. I so wished now that I should have controlled my desire back then.

'I have not come here to share my whereabouts.'

'You seem angry with me, sir.'

I could see fear in her eyes and knew the reason behind this fear. 'How would you define our relationship?'

'You are my favourite teacher.'

She had said the right thing.

'Then what made everyone talk about our *more than friends* status?'

'We are girlfriend-boyfriend! Are we not?'

This was not going anywhere. She did not understand the logic of love and lust. I thanked myself for not being involved with her any more than I was. I tried to moderate the intensity of my anger and requested her to sit. Ordering a cup of natural mango ice cream for her, I asked, 'Did I ever say that I loved you?'

She thought for a few seconds, 'No.'

'Have I ever said we would be good as a couple or girlfriend and boyfriend?'

'But what is the problem? If… suppose… we think in that direction…?'

I took a deep breath. Deep breaths help to control the mind. I emptied the glass of water in front of me and used a tissue to wipe my lips. Ananya was silent. She had stopped licking her favourite ice-cream.

'I am eleven years elder to you. Currently I'm jobless… we do not have any future.'

'Not in a job means…?' Her response was not what I had anticipated

'I am on notice period because you… or your family member complained about me… that I molested you in my staff quarters.'

'Oh! And no, my family never made the complaint,' she shook her head vehemently.

'Then who did?'

She shrugged. That's all. As if that was all she could do about a punishment that came to me because of her in the first place. She was lost in her own assumptions and said things that mattered only to her, not really answering me.

'Sir, could you help me in getting 11th final exam papers? Math is the toughest subject. If you don't help me, then I will fail.'

'When did I say that I may have access to the paper and I would share them with you?' I asked incredulously.

I got an understanding of something which was another aspect of the human behaviour. 'You have come to me because of those exam papers?'

She was so lost in herself, she did not reply. But she didn't even deny it. Sometimes absence of denial is also acceptance.

'You know, I did not top the class just because of maths,' she said, as if admitting to something shameful.

I held my head. My life was at a crux and this girl was talking of unimportant things like maths papers and topping in school exams.

'Well done, sir!'

Her tone was like a movie climax's dialogue when everyone starts to clap just to support the main character. I didn't reply to her sarcasm.

'You used me and now you have found a new girlfriend,' she said with teenage anger bubbling around her.

'Used you! Are you insane? And who is my new girlfriend?'

'Don't act innocent! The same girl whose house you've happily shifted in.' She looked away, I thought in disgust, and I didn't know what to say to this childish behaviour.

'Pihu...?' Incredulous!

She nodded.

'She is not my girlfriend!'

'Stop taking me for a fool, sir. The entire school knows about her. She has had her eye on you forever. She always talks about you, even though you never taught her. And now you have shifted with her, in her own house!' Ananya's tone was accusatory.

'I don't want to get into any discussion. But there is nothing between Pihu and me. Is that clear?' I raised my voice.

'Oh yeah? Then why did she complain about me?'

'She complained... about you... for what?'

'Principal ma'am called me to her office. I found out Pihu had complained that I was getting tuitions from a teacher. I saw the complaint letter as well. She clearly mentioned my name, but there was no mention of your name, *sir*,' she ended sarcastically.

I was shocked. It was Pihu! Oh god, that girl had almost ruined me. And here I was, thinking she had been great help.

'And from where did Pihu find out that you were getting tuitions?'

She hesitated, shifting her focus to the ice-cream.

I understood her discomfort. 'Can you please tell me from where she got to know about our little study arrangement?'

'I might have uttered it… in a heated argument.' She could not see me in the eyes.

'Could you elaborate what the argument was about? And why name was dragged into it?'

'Pihu was asking about you, so I said, you and I were friends. She began arguing… for no reason. She was unstoppable. I was so fed up of her prattling… just to shut her up I told her you were giving tuitions to me.'

I rolled my eyes in anger, confusion and disgust, each emotion competing with the other to be on top. 'Let me clear one thing, you are not my girlfriend. In fact, there is nothing between you and me.'

She did not reply.

'Is that clear, Ananya?' I asked sternly.

She looked at me for a few seconds and gave a sarcastic smile. 'Congratulations on your new and sick girlfriend.'

Twenty-two

I clenched my teeth, but my body continued to shake. When I got to know that Pihu was the one who had complained about me, in all seriousness, I wanted to kill her. This was height of her obsession with me! The girl did not have brains. I stormed home and the word came out almost as a scream, 'Pihuuuu!'

I knew Annu would not be at home. Pihu came out within seconds, looking confused.

I blasted, 'You complained about me and...' I was not comfortable including Ananya's name. Pihu's face still had an innocent immature smile, which was now unbearable for me.

'I did not complain about my favourite teacher.' She had clearly not understood the question.

I reframed it. 'Did you write about anyone or anything at school?'

'Yes, I wrote a letter about Ananya,' she answered simply.

'What did you say?'

'I mentioned that I also wanted tuitions. Why was only she allowed?' she said, as if she had not been granted a holiday which everyone else was enjoying.

'Do you know it's because of you that I have been thrown out of the accommodation?'

'How is asking permission for tuitions... related to you?' Her innocence made it click. I realised, it could not have been because of Pihu's letter. She had only spoken about tuition.

The accusations must have been cooked up by the frustrated teachers who were jealous of me. I was thrown out of the campus because they guessed and had their own conclusions of what was going on inside the room. Pihu was the one who offered me shelter when I was thrown out and had nowhere to go. She was really always trying to help.

Before I could forgive her and ask for forgiveness for being rude, she committed another blunder.

'Ananya is not a good girl.' Pihu made a face.

'I do not want your opinion about her or about anything.'

'She was spreading rumours about you, sir.'

'Rumours... what rumours?'

'That you were sharing question papers with her.'

It was a roller coaster of unbelievable things today! Pihu had been aware about everything... every damn thing. Yet she offered me her house to live in?

'Can I ask you one question, Pihu?'

She nodded, her smile turning bigger.

'Why did you offer me a place to stay here... in your house?'

She hesitated, then smiled foolishly, without any reason and vomited the same shit that I was so tired of hearing. 'Because you are my favourite teacher.'

▼

A mother can never accept that her daughter is fishing for a man who is eleven years older to her. A landlord would not digest a tenant indulging with a family member, and no one can bear to see a bad person around themselves.

I had a new problem to worry about – what if Annu found out her daughter's obsession for a teacher?

It had become a routine for us to meet on Saturdays. I was on the terrace, strolling, when Annu made her appearance around midnight. Her half-sleeved t-shirt and the long track pants were quite modest. She was expecting me here.

Our eyes met. Her lips curved into a smile. It was not the most beautiful smile in this world, but it said a lot. It was the smile of a person who, no matter what the situation, refused to give up. I have never noticed anything like this in other people before. Why did I have a different outlook towards her, I don't know. But I could even sense an unsaid burden of duty on her.

We exchanged smiles, but I tried to keep my eagerness to talk to her in check.

'Neel, is everything okay? You look tensed.'

'Nothing, just worried about the job…'

'It will all be fine.' She said the good words and went to her customary corner.

I left my corner and walked to her, my eyes on the river. I stopped a few steps away from her, considering our situation. Two adults staring at the Mula river, as if the river was going to adopt us.

I was still framing the hard-hitting question in my head when she broke the silence, 'So you wish to ask something?'

'Do you read minds?' I let out the tensed breath I had been holding.

'Are you worried about Ananya?'

I swallowed my own saliva to wet my suddenly dry throat. My eyes widened as I stared harder at her. I gave her a guarded, cajoling puppy dog smile as I said, 'Yes… a bit… I was thinking about Ananya.'

Why was Pihu not as good as her mother at understanding people? If she had even a little understanding of my discomfort because of one fault of hers, my life would be so much easier.

'Well? How is she? Everything resolved?'

I did not understand what she meant by 'resolved', but she had raised the wrong topic. 'Yes, all resolved.' I nodded to finish it off.

She looked at me squarely. Was I suddenly more interesting than the river?

I understood her curiosity. She wanted to know more about Ananya. I had to bring up what was in my head, 'Can I ask you something, Annu?'

'Go on.'

'Do you know the actual reason because of which I was thrown out of the staff quarters?'

'Yes… I think so. I have heard the rumours.'

Frankly speaking, I was not sure how I could ask her… about how much she knew. The word "rumours" rang in my ears. Maybe she did not know the entire story. I gathered some more courage by swallowing another lump of my saliva. 'And you still allowed me to stay at your house?'

'I am a progressive woman,' she replied confidently. 'I have nothing to do with your personal life.'

My interest to win the landlord's heart was demolished with that statement. She did not want to be personal with me.

135

I nodded.

'Can I ask you one personal question?' I asked. This line is the master foot note. After this, you can ask anything.

She frowned, then nodded.

'If you do not wish to answer, you can ignore it,' I offered. 'Just out of curiosity, why does Pihu hate Dr Vedant?'

She smiled. She had a glow on her face, as if a teenager had asked a grown up about their crush.

'She thinks I am having an affair with Dr Vedant,' she replied.

I did not say anything. A frown on my forehead and a question mark on the face conveyed that I was expecting an explanation.

'Well… Dr Vedant works in Birla Hospital. He is a very good doctor. I visit his home for some personal help. It makes Pihu feel like we have some equation…' She shook her head offering a defensive smile. '…Dr Vedant is happily married and blessed with two healthy kids.'

I nodded and thought I should not delve deeper into the matter. 'Can I ask you… one more personal question…?'

She gave me a look. I must be getting too personal. Her openness had allowed me to take the risk. 'I see you here… almost every Saturday. You spend your time in isolation. I understand your situation. You cannot share all aspects of your life… with Pihu. Why have you not decided to…?' I lacked the courage to finish the sentence. I guessed, I had said enough.

'Who will marry a liability?' she responded without hesitation, almost as a reflex.

'Liability?'

'Nothing.' She shook her head, dismissing some thought. 'Nothing… Forget I said anything.'

'You couldn't think of your child as a liability…'

'It's not about Pihu as a daughter. It is… it's something else.' Her lips were drawn in a thin line.

I couldn't bring myself to ask any more. I felt, I had crossed some boundary, so I stopped right there.

'One thing, sir.'

She had come back to "sir" now. I guessed my question had hurt her.

'…the reason I allowed you in our home was… Pihu loves you. And she believes…'

'Believes what?'

'Since she is a kid, she believes in a story of an angel and a demon. An angel who fixes everything.'

'So…?'

'She believes you are her angel.'

Twenty-three

Exams were over, the school was off for two months, and the students were also enjoying their time. I was happy, because I could finally avoid the useless and unproductive private tuition for some days.

I was strolling in the garden when I saw something unusual. I did a double take when I watched her walk out. Pihu was a painful sight in red and flesh. The edge of her dress just grazed her thighs. As my eyes travelled up her thread doll figure, I could see much more than just her neckline. And from the broad cut, I was sure, not much of the back was also covered. Her pale complexion was even more pronounced by the red lipstick she wore. Her high heels, thin naked legs made looking impossible for me. I was definitely repelled by the unwaxed legs she was flaunting. I had to look at her again to make sure I was seeing right.

'Where are you going?'

'My friend's birthday party… at her home,' she answered gleefully.

'Great,' was all I could say.

'How am I looking?'

'Beautiful! You have dressed up like this...,' I looked at her from top to bottom, '...only for a home party?'

'Why... you have any problem with this dress?'

'Why should I have any problem with your dress?'

'You can shout at me... if you think it's not good.'

'What nonsense!' I wanted to say more, but Annu's image flashed in my mind. 'Are you waiting for someone?'

'Yes, for the cab. It must be on the way.'

'Oh, so the party is somewhere far?'

'No. She lives here in Baner... this society only... near Park Express Road.'

Park Express Road was just five hundred meters away from the house. Who would possibly need a vehicle for that distance! I had had too much of Pihu's life. Her strange and unpredictable behaviour was beyond me.

139

'What happened to your father, Pihu?' I asked a direct question, not bothering with pleasantries and considerations of politeness.

'My father passed away due to a blood infection... it has been nearly five years now.' Pihu responded openly.

'Do you have any memory of him? How was he?'

The immature smile vanished from her face. She went silent. It was a difficult question for any child.

'Sorry... I don't know why I brought that up,' I apologised.

She did not say anything.

I had to think of something, quick to divert her mind. I came up with another thoughtless query. 'Why don't you go for tuitions like others do? Maybe to a professional coaching institute....' I shrugged. This query could help me get rid of her too.

'Because I can't take the stress.'

'All girls of your age go out. You always stay here, at home…
just to avoid stress?' I looked at her exasperatedly.

'Yes,' she answered in a small voice.

I wanted to say something, but her sad face made me shut
up.

'Take care then, don't take stress.' I moved away with the
sarcastic words.

'Thank you for the concern, sir. You are really sweet,' she
replied with a smile,

▼

140

It was Saturday evening again. I had come up with another set
of questions and was waiting for Annu to come to the terrace. I
no longer needed the excuse of being tensed or wanting fresh
air. Annu and I had become friends enough to ask personal
questions.

She walked in, as anticipated, when the darkness deepened,
and things got quiet. Devoid of any make-up, her skin looked
youthful and fresh. Her hair blew softly in the breeze while
occasionally the moonlight illuminated her glossy lips. I had by
now memorized the contours of her face and could fill in what
could not be seen in the darkness. She was always beautiful.

We exchanged a welcome smile. She moved to her favourite
corner. I spent some time walking aimlessly, before my legs took
me to her.

'Hi Neel, how are you?'

So we were back to my name now. Good!

'I am good. And thanks for the job reference at the coaching institute.'

'Oh, don't mention it! Do you still have any formalities left at school?'

'I have to visit next Friday. I have already discharged my responsibilities, just need to submit a few books and fill the no dues form.'

'Is it painful to leave school, at this point?'

'Indeed, it is.'

'Can understand...'

Her sympathy for me lasted a few minutes, then she turned back to her riveting conversation with the night's fresh air.

Queries were badgering my mind. I had to ask her. I looked at her twice. But she stood devotedly like a saint. After hovering for ten minutes, I gave up the idea of asking anything.

She broke the silence, 'You wished to ask something... personal?'

This was epic! I wondered if she was a psychologist. How could she know so precisely what I was thinking... every single time? Was my dazed face enough for her to know? Or was it just that I was repetitive?

'Feel free to ask, Neel.'

'I wished to ask a few things, about Pihu?'

'Has she done something wrong?'

'Why does she not mix with other students? She never goes out with her friends. Won't this turn her into an introvert? She will not be able to keep up with others... normal, growing children,' I said in one go.

She did not look shocked. I realized, she was not facing

these questions for the first time. I expected her to not be too forthcoming with any explanation.

'I know she requires a lot of exposure. Even her IQ is low...'

'You are her mom, you should not be so protective of her...'

'Actually...you are right. I will try to take care.' She hesitated a little.

I was seriously concerned for Annu, or for that matter even Pihu. It was a chance to sympathise with a mom who loved her daughter, to advance my own interests.

'What happened?' I said softly. 'Is there something you want to share?'

'No. But, thanks for your concern for Pihu.'

She did not give away anything. All I got was that practical "thanks". There was delicate information, floating in the air, just beyond my grasp. It seemed, everyone knew it, but no one talked about it.

Twenty-four

I stood staring at the few five-hundred-rupee notes in the drawer. Six thousand rupees, that was all I had in my cupboard. My ATM account had already dried out. I had not received any salary in the last two months. School was closed and so were the coaching centres.

Where from could I arrange money? I sagged on the bed. I could not ask for any more financial help from mom. I had to think. It was not happening for the first time, after all. I had faced similar crisis before.

I had not paid a single rupee as rent till now. I assumed, either these people were too generous and never asked for rent, or maybe they were just fools.

I looked around the room. I could sell something, I thought. Images of a gold chain began dancing in front of my eyes. That thick gold chain sure had some pleasant memories. I had stolen it from Neha, while she had been by my side, after one of our ardent encounters. I pulled out the precious chain from the bag. It gleamed as I felt it between my fingers. I had a warm feeling for my emergency backup money, so I pampered it. It could easily fetch me close to one lakh rupees.

I picked the chain up. It was a matter of my survival now. It was time to sell it.

Breaking my chain of thoughts about the chain, my phone rang.

'Hi, is this Mr Neel?' the unknown caller asked.

It gave me chills when someone asked for me like that! I tried to think of the person whose life I could have possibly spoilt.

'Yes...'

'We are calling from DAV School, accounts department. Your full and final settlement is ready. You can collect the cheque on any working day.'

The lady's cheerful voice brought a ray of hope to my bleak life. 'Can I come now?'

'Yes, Mr Neel. You definitely can.'

I went to collect my salary which the school had been holding during my notice period.

Aarav was waiting for me. I had called him just after I had received the call. I told you, he was a rare friend. I don't know how he always managed to find time for me.

At the accounts counter, a bored looking lady handed me an envelope. My relieving letter read—

TO WHOMSOEVER IT MAY CONCERN

Mr Neel Kumar has been discharged from his duties at DAV Private School. He worked as Post Graduate Teacher (Maths).

He resigned on his own and his conduct was good during the job.

Regards,
Human resource
DAV Private School

To this feeling-less letter, they had attached a cheque for forty-two thousand rupees. I heaved a sigh of relief. The amount was enough to tide me over comfortably for the next three months or so.

There was only one person at the school who I could call a friend. He came to bid me farewell. We were sitting in the canteen, waiting. This was probably the last time I was sitting with him, in school premises.

'How are you feeling, Neel?'

I never get attached to anyone, but today I was a little upset as Aarav was the saddest I had ever seen him.

'Hey, Aarav, I am happy. I don't need to sell my rainy-day backup gold chain anymore. Cheer up, man!'

He frowned, but sat still. There was disappointment all over his face. He must have been expecting a little more emotion from me.

'The same chain which you stole from your sister-in-law?'

'Yes,' I replied with a sly smile.

'How is your love triangle shaping up?' he changed the topic intentionally.

'Love triangle...?' I looked at him blankly.

'Yes, just like in the movies... Pihu loves Neel, who is eleven years elder than her. And Neel likes Annu, Pihu's mom, who again, is eleven years elder to him.'

'Did I not tell you, I don't like this game? I am not enjoying this anymore.' I was quite affected with this topic.

'Why, what happened?' he prodded.

'Nothing yaar! Everything is fine. It's just... just that I feel... uncomfortable because of Pihu. She has this larger than life image of mine...'

'As in?'

'She believes that I am an angel.' I said

'Angel...' he giggled. 'Mr Angel Neel Kumar.' He laughed out loud.

This was the first time he had laughed today.

'Give me a break!' I shook my head.

'Okay... Let's forget Pihu for the moment. What do we do about her mother now? What next?' Aarav asked enthusiastically.

'I am waiting for the day when I find her at the lowest. She would be hurting, and I would lend her a shoulder to cry on...'

'You moron! You still think you can win her over?' Aarav slammed the table.

'Do not underestimate the power of good looks,' I smiled slyly, exhibiting myself as the best-looking man on earth.

'But what about you and Pihu?' Aarav burst my bubble.

'She is an immature girl. A nuisance. I don't care about her,' I said disparagingly.

'Can I ask you something?' Aarav looked straight at me, almost emotionless.

I looked up at him.

'You do not have friends, no family… you never cared for Ananya. And now… not even Pihu. What in life do you care for?'

'I care for you,' I said seriously.

But he had known this to be my best evading tactic till date.

'Stop this nonsense, Neel. And stop playing with Annu's emotions!'

It was unexpected. Why was my only friend suddenly taking someone else's side? He looked really upset. I always thought he was like me. Now it looked like, I was wrong. He was far better than me.

He took a long breath and said. 'I want to show you a picture.'

'Any new good-looking girl?'

'Look at this!' He placed his mobile phone close to my nose.

I moved a little forward to have a better look at the image. It was my photo in a black formal coat. But the picture was hazy, like the original print was made years ago.

'From where did you get such an old picture of mine? I don't even remember when it was clicked.' I looked at him confused, then at the picture.

'It's not you… look carefully.'

I narrowed my eyes. Was that not me? No, it was not. I don't remember having dressed like that, ever.

'Who is this guy?' I asked Aarav, puzzled.

'This, my dear friend, is Mr Mangesh!' Aarav answered as if he was extracting a live rabbit from his hat of tricks.

'How do you know? Where did you get this picture from?'

'That is not the point! This is your answer to why Annu was soft on you… allowing you to live in her house without rent.'

I turned back to the mobile. I zoomed into the picture, not sure what I was trying to see. It was me there, wearing a black blazer, the lips curving, trying to achieve a professional smile. It appeared plastic. The face was similar to mine, but I knew, that was not me in that outfit.

My cunning mind was already churning. Many things were revealing themselves. Why Annu used to stare at me whenever we met, why she had let me live in her house, even after knowing everything…

'I look like Mangesh…' I smiled, then laughed, and said, 'I look just like her husband.'

Twenty-five

Everyone in Pune waited for July, because it brought rains. It was perfect weather. I was enjoying my evening tea and considering reading a romantic book. The best part of reading a romantic book was how real it felt. You could feel everything happening around you. Before I could reach for my book pile, there was a rattle at the door. The intensity of the noise confirmed it was Pihu. I wondered what I could do.

I opened the door.

'Hi, sir, hope you were not sleeping.'

'No, I was....'

She walked in, asking in her signature style, 'May I be allowed to come inside?'

'You are already inside the room.'

'Sir, will you play Carrom?'

'No, I am not interested...'

She made a face and sat on the chair.

'Why don't you play with your friends, or with your mom?'

'I do not have friends, and mom is not at home. Anyway, I am fed up of playing with her. I want to play with you.'

She said authoritatively, as if I was born with the moral obligation to play Carrom or Ludo with her. I stared at her. There was innocence on her face and I could see she was bored. Loneliness is the biggest enemy a person can have. Frankly speaking, I am not so modest that I would entertain a kid's whim, but I guess I too was getting bored.

'Would you happen to have a bat and ball?'

'Yes, of course,' she replied excitedly.

She almost ran out of the room. I had never seen her move so fast. She returned after nearly ten minutes with a plastic bat and ball in her hands. She would have barely taken thirty steps, but it appeared she had just run a marathon. She was trying hard to catch her breath. I felt irritated. How could someone be so weak? This was the result of over-pampering kids, not allowing them to play and keeping them confined to their rooms.

'Are you alright?' I asked, barely able to hide my sarcasm.

'Let's play!' she said cheerfully.

'You play with a plastic bat?'

'Yes.' She coughed.

I had stopped playing with plastic bats and balls when I was in class third.

'Sir, let's start the game. Mom will be coming anytime.'

'Would you like to bat first?' I guessed fielding would be difficult for her.

She agreed happily.

We drew a few wriggly lines on the boundary wall; that was going to be our wicket. I made a rule. We had to run to earn every run.

I bowled my first ball. Swinging the bat was an effort for her. I made ten deliveries and understood, I was playing with a five-years-old. She carried on like a slow-motion movie, and it only went slower with every delivery. I cursed myself for having decided to play with her. It was better to die of boredom.

'Are you done?' I asked.

'Yes, now your turn to bat.'

'No, I am okay.' I did not wish to prolong my torture.

'No, sir. I am a good bowler.'

'Really?'

She nodded, looking more like a dead athlete.

I stepped on to my batting crease. Holding the plastic bat with one hand, I looped it between my fingers. It was hard to imagine, how Pihu could even pretend it was heavy. She picked the ball, ran two feet, and threw the ball towards me. It bounced three times before reaching me. This game wouldn't last long!

'I think you could show some more strength.'

She nodded.

Collecting all her strength, she made her next delivery. I hit the ball. She ran like a turtle and collected the ball. She crawled to collect the next ball I hit.

'Run fast, dear, else you will lose the game!' I shouted, trying to pump a little energy.

She nodded, took a long breath, and threw the ball again. With every delivery, I secured two runs.

'Fast, Pihu! You are slow.'

She nodded again, trying to catch her breath. Summoning all her courage, she was about to throw the ball, but began panting.

151

She attempted to regulate her breathing, but collapsed onto the ground.

For seconds, I watched, puzzled. Curious, I moved towards her, collected her onto my lap and tried to shake her into consciousness.

Pihu remained quiet. She was almost unconscious, her eyes only half open. She was breathing roughly.

I called out her name loudly, 'Pihu... Pihu! Come on...'

But she did not reply. I watched her eyes close shut. A chill ran through my body. I tried to think. Should I call Annu? What would I tell her?

Should I get some water to splash on her face? I couldn't leave her here... I suddenly felt helpless. I was used to the Pihu who ordered me around. I did not know how to handle this listless, quiet Pihu in my arms. Pictures flashed in front of my eyes while she remained motionless. My brain failed to react. '... I must call Annu...,' I mumbled to myself, pulling out my phone.

Putting the phone against my ears, I looked around in panic. The phone slipped from my hand in relief. I opened my mouth to explain what had happened. Annu came and stood there, white as a ghost.

I heard her hollow voice, 'How long has my daughter been lying here?'

Twenty-six

She did not ask what had happened. I was scared to even offer an apology. Annu was an efficient nurse. She was calm... too calm for my comfort. As if she had seen this happen many times. Of course, she would have, she was a nurse, but she was also a mother. She asked me to help her carry Pihu to bed. While I made sure Pihu was lying comfortably, Annu came up with a loaded syringe. Her face looked like it had been carved out of stone as she punctured her daughter's skin with the long needle. Then she checked her pulse. She was absolutely silent, no expression, no emotion, not an extra movement.

I couldn't take the silence, 'Sorry... about this. It... it all happened so suddenly I couldn't cal...'

'It's okay.' She cut me off. Her words were heartless.

She was not interested in hearing me out. For her, I might as well could have been invisible.

She moved away from the bed and made a call. She listened to the person on the other end and disconnected. Pulling out a stethoscope, she started digging on her daughter's chest. She noted something on a plane paper. Maybe a doctor would understand what she was doing. I only knew she was upset. I regretted having accepted Pihu's invitation to play.

'Shall we call the doctor?' I heard my voice in the quiet room.

There was no reply.

This was an utter overreaction! Why was she acting like this? I genuinely felt sorry. Not so much for Pihu, but a mother who was managing everything on her own. I did not miss the fact that she was trying hard to not cry. She was struggling with the torrent of emotions.

'Is there anything I could help you with?' I was now rapidly feeling sorry for myself.

Her expression hardened. 'Thank you, not required.'

I had no option but to leave the place. As I came down the stairs, I saw Dr Vednat's car smoothly coming to a halt outside the gate. He walked past me without a glance at me. Before the door closed, I heard him enquiring, 'How is Pihu...?'

▼

It was a long night for all of us. Ever since I had found out I looked like Annu's husband, I had felt a strange excitement. Now, suddenly, everything had taken a turn for the worst. Annu's attitude was killing me. Why did she zone me out? She could have questioned me, blamed me, or shouted at me... Sometimes, silence hurts the most. A mother's silence is the loudest scream.

It was late. I tossed on the bed several times before giving it up. I found myself taking the steps to the terrace. I had met Annu there on many occasions, but today, her presence was a surprise.

The tension of her body gave away how upset she was. She stood gazing at the river as if it had the power to heal all wounds, fresh and old.

She must have realised she was no longer alone, but she ignored my presence. Deep in my stomach, I felt guilty.

I strolled aimlessly. I wanted to talk to her, but was hesitant after the cold behaviour of a few hours back. Plus, she was preoccupied with her daughter's health. I asked myself, *"What was I even doing here? She needed Mangesh... not Neel."* Mangesh, who I look like. I felt a surge of strange confidence. Yes, it was me, who by some strange coincidence looked like her husband.

'Annu, how is Pihu?'

'She is conscious. She is doing fine now,' she said coldly.

Her tone clarified her disinterest in any conversation with me. I slowly walked to the other end of the terrace. All I could think of was how I could restart the conversation.

From the corner of my eyes, I saw her wiping her face. She had been crying. There was no sound, but I could see a mother shedding tears.

I watched her for some seconds, then walked towards her. 'Annu, are you okay?'

'Yes, Neel. I am.'

I stood there helplessly, but could not let go. 'Annu, I am sure it's nothing. Pihu will be fine... everything will be fine.'

'No, noting would be fine,' she said almost in a whisper, holding back a scream, it felt.

The tear-soaked silence told me something was terribly wrong with Annu. I wanted to comfort her. Moving to her side,

I stood beside her, our sides nearly touching, but not quite. 'Is there any way I can help you?'

'No… no one can help me.'

She burst into a fresh stretch of tears, covering her face. I felt bad for the lonely woman whom I had always seen to be strong and confident. Truth was, I still did not know a lot about her. I was still far from reality. I felt sympathy, but no deeper emotion. Her sobs were still distressing the night around us. After moments of hesitation, I put my hands on her shoulders, to console her. Even if I was a stranger, I could not see her crying. I was surprised at my own sensitive side, and she did not seem to mind my gesture.

'I have lost everything, Neel. I've lost everything…' her sobs caught in her throat.

I could not take the pain in her voice. I pulled her close, hugging her to me, trying to comfort her. It seemed to help her, because she hugged me tighter. I had always dreamt of this moment, but not in such a situation. My closeness might have helped, but it did not stop her tears, '…I've lost everything…' she repeated.

'Don't talk like that, Annu. I am sure it's nothing. Have faith, everything will be fine…'

'No… it's not *nothing*. It's my daughter… my Pihu…'

'Yes! Pihu will be fine… She is a brave girl.'

I had had no idea what Annu had been going through. Why so much pain in her voice. Then she said something that made the situation abundantly clear.

'Neel, Pihu is dying…'

Twenty-seven

Pihu's Mother Speaks

Thanks, Neel, for giving me an opportunity to talk about her. Frankly speaking, I did not wish to write about Pihu... her situation. But I think, now, my version of the story is necessary.

The only love of my life, my Pihu, was born with a blood disorder. Her father was a thalassemia patient, and she got it from her father. Sadly, it was the worst thing she could have gotten from such a gentle, nice man. Pihu was a beta thalassemia patient.

If you wonder what that means, thalassemia is an inherited blood disorder in which the body makes an abnormal form of haemoglobin. Someone could have alpha thalassemia, beta thalassemia, or thalassemia minor. Thalassemia major, however, is the severest form of beta thalassemia. It develops when beta-globin genes are missing. The symptoms of thalassemia major generally appear before a child's second birthday.

I discovered about her disease when she was three years old. I have been in the medical line long enough to know it is fatal.

As she grew up, I cajoled Pihu into believing she shouldn't stress herself, but hid the truth from her. I never told her about her father's illness. I felt, if she found out she had inherited the disease from her father, she would not love him like she does now.

Mangesh and I had been in love, so we got married. I worked as a nurse in Aditya Birla hospital. He visited regularly, and those visits made us friends. I did not notice when that friendship bloomed into love.

Those days, thalassemia was not a known disease. I lost Mangesh when Pihu was in class sixth. Pihu's memories with her father are the best memories for me. But living in the present with old memories is like scratching your wounds each day. After all, memories are a gift and a curse.

It was hard to see my love go, snatched from me, right in front of my eyes. I was so helpless in spite of being a medical practitioner. I got help and support from everyone – family, friends, colleagues. But it was my pain that could not be shared. Not even with my daughter.

Pihu was closer to her father, always. Even when we knew we should take control of the situation and make her less dependent on him, I couldn't do it. It would have been cruel to them both. After Mangesh left, it was difficult for her to sleep on many nights. She often asked when her papa would come. I am her mother; I tried to handle the situation. To comfort her, I told her a story – an illogical, stupid story of an angel and a demon. I told her, a demon had taken her father away.

She used to ask how we would get the happiness back. And I said, '…one day, an angel will come, and a miracle will happen….'

I know it was a stupid and unrealistic idea. But it worked. She started believing that the angel exists, and miracles do happen.

I didn't have courage to tell her that… there are no angels in real life. She had limited number of days to live. I decided to let her live those days with the myth. How could I deny my baby the tiny hope in her little life?

It was difficult for me to know that the child I had given life to, was about to lose it, and I still had to live with a brave face. All I could do was take care of Pihu and I did that with all my heart and soul.

The regular visits to the doctor found me a friend in Dr Vedant. In spite of being aware of Dr Vedant's doubtful intentions, I still maintained my friendship with him. I have had to go out on dates with him, despite knowing that he is a married man, because he is a good doctor. I don't have the kind of money which I needed for Pihu's regular treatment, just for her to survive. Dr Vedant was not charging me any fee. It was an unsaid agreement between him and me. I had to compromise with a lot… but I had no choice.

Usually, beta thalassemia patients live for about twelve or fourteen years. But Dr Vedant has done a good job in giving my daughter the best treatment. It has made her live for some more years… to endure her pain for some more time.

Modern research has made beta thalassemia major curable by Bone Marrow Transplant (BMT). Worldwide, thousands of children have undergone the procedure. If it is successful, the patient would no longer need blood transfusions. We tried to find a donor in the family for Pihu, by some linked procedure… but her body did not support it.

Initially, Pihu needed blood transfusion in six months, but of late, she has needed it on monthly basis. I knew she was heading to her destiny, and there wasn't much I could do.

All I have in this world is my job as a nurse, and this house located in this posh society which my husband has left me. I have Pihu, but she will not be with me for much longer. It kills me to watch my child getting closer to death every day. They say pain makes you stronger, but I don't know if I will live to see any more. Just the thought of Pihu going away from me breaks my heart to pieces. I have long since stopped believing in god. I just try to find a quiet place to cry, which mostly is the secluded spot on the terrace.

Pihu is not allowed to stress herself, leave aside play like a normal child. I have stopped forcing Pihu for anything. Why to put extra stress on her in her short life. I didn't make her work on her studies, which has made her weak. She has failed several times, but no exam is tougher than the exam she is facing in life. I try to give her all that she wishes for, which has made her a little stubborn too.

One day, she called me up and seemed fixated on the idea of renting our house to some teacher in her school, by the name Neel. I was dead against a teacher staying in our house, even on rent. Because nobody knows about her condition there, and I didn't want Pihu being a subject of peoples' and other students' pity and sympathy now. But this girl was hell-bent on helping her favourite teacher. I decided, I could throw him out within a day or two even if I say yes now.

But I had to change my mind as soon as I saw Neel. He looked exactly like Mangesh, my husband. He had the same eyes, the same nose, even their smiles are the same.

Neel is a good man. He agreed to give tuitions to Pihu for free. I heard he had been thrown out of the school because he was giving tuitions to another girl Ananya... or maybe Ananya and Neel were more involved than that. Frankly speaking, I had nothing to do with his past. Gradually, I started liking him... more and more. He took interest in my life, and I found a good friend in him. Pihu got to spend quality time with him. They played a few indoor games when I was late at work. Pihu was extremely happy with Neel around. I was happy that Pihu was loved by such a caring man. When I shared my pain with Neel, he hugged me and consoled me... like a true friend would.

But I have another confession to make. I had started liking him. I often wondered why a man who looked so similar to my husband had come into my life and was taking care of the family. Do angels really exist? I was certain Neel was here to make things right. I believe, Neel is the angel.

161

Twenty-eight

Pretending to be happy when you're in pain says tons about how strong you are as a person. Annu spoke her heart out, standing at the corner of the terrace in my arms.

And suddenly, everything started falling into place. This was exactly what I had wanted to know all these days. Yes, it was not a situation that I would have chosen, not even for Pihu... but did I really care?

In the past, every night, I only used to see an attractive woman on the terrace. I failed to see her silent tears. Pain of the mind is worse than the pain of the body. I realised... why Pihu was a liability.... Why Vedant was so close to Annu... and why Pihu hated Vedant.

I had sympathy for a mother, and understanding of why Pihu was the way she was. And honestly, it was a strange feeling to know that these two women had far too much trust and belief in me. I felt suddenly burdened with unsaid responsibilities, hopes and commitments. These were new feelings. I had never till now felt the power of responsibility.

Since I was feeling genuinely worried for them, I went up to see them a few hours later. Now I could walk into their flat any time, because I wasn't the outsider anymore. Annu opened the door and welcomed me inside.

'How is Pihu?' I asked one simple question, holding in it several others.

Annu pointed me towards her room, so that I could have a look myself. I went to Pihu's room. She lay in bed, eyes closed. I sat on a chair on the bedside. Is this silly girl really going to die? I thought. And it was a strange feeling. Maybe because I had never seen someone on their deathbed before. Annu was busy in the kitchen. She had taken the day off. While I was there, Pihu opened her eyes.

'How are you, Pihu?'

She was delighted to see me.

'I am bored,' she responded.

'Nothing can be done. You need to rest.'

'Yes, I have been hearing that since forever.' She tried to roll her eyes, but got tired of that too.

'Would you like to play Ludo?' I asked, just to make her feel good.

'No, I don't want to play anything...' She said seriously which tensed me up a bit. I had asked for a bat and ball, and my guilt was at its peak looking at her like that. '...Can I ask a question?' she asked and broke my reverie.

The beauty of Pihu was, whether you give her permission to ask a question or not, she would still ask. It was weird seeing her so serious, though.

'Will you miss me?'

Any reply to that question was pointless. Even in this state, her obsession was strangely high.

'I have to leave, dear, you take care,' I said and got up to go.

'Come on, sir. I will get bored.'

'You need to rest, Pihu.'

'You should spend some time with me. You may miss me tomorrow.' She said in a soft but matter of fact voice.

'What does that mean?'

'I am dying… soon.' She said lightly, with a smile. How could she, she was just seventeen.

'Are you not afraid of dea…?'

'I am more afraid that you will forget me.'

Here was this strange, weird… amateurish girl, who wanted to register herself in history.

'You are not so easy to forget Pihu. You are a girl to remember.'
She passed a contented smile.

'What do you want me to do, Pihu? So that you don't get bored. Tell me!' I did not know what else to say.

'Could you please tell me a story…?'

'Umm, okay! Which story do you like?'

'A love story, of an angel and a demon.'

I looked at her, she was smiling. I don't know what that smile was stirring in me. Perhaps a part of me I had never known before, wanted to tell her a story… the story she wanted to hear. 'I promise Pihu, one day… I will tell you a story.'

Twenty-nine

Aarav and I sat at Ozone, our favourite food joint, enjoying the rabri-jalebi. This place serves Pune's best jalebi and super tasty rabri. Aarav ordered one plate and offered to pay. He knew that I had no job and was on a limited budget.

'I cannot understand what kind of a girl she is,' Aarav said emphatically.

'Are all these things happening for real?' I shook my head.

'Where is the doubt?' Aarav stuffed his mouth with half a jalebi.

'Annu is eleven years older than me, and Pihu is eleven years younger to me. I like Annu, while Pihu likes me. And Pihu is dying. Is this not a filmy story?'

'This is not a filmy story, but did you think of yourself as a hero?' Aarav smirked.

'I am really worried about the whole situation. Or maybe because I am jobless, I have spent too much time on these useless issues,' I said resignedly.

'How is the job search coming? Any interview calls?'

'Nothing yaar… the coaching institutes will start next week. Anyway, they are paying a meagre two hundred rupees per hour. It's not enough to sustain. I have to find another job soon.'

The lip-smacking jalebi plate lay empty between us. Aarav came to the actual point of why he had called this meeting.

'I am sending you details of a school on WhatsApp. They require a Maths teacher for eighth and ninth standards.'

My eyes widened with interest, 'Wow! This is great. Which school?'

'St Anthony School, Goa!' Aarav beamed.

I did not even thank him for forwarding my CV and referring me to the school.

'Why Goa? They don't have a branch in Pune?'

'How does that matter? You have any location preference?'

I did not offer any more explanation. I knew he would be displeased. I had long made up my mind that Aarav was an emotional fool. Here I was, wishing to own the ocean, and my friend was offering me a tiny fish.

'No, actually… I don't want to leave Pune.'

Fools always treat themselves as the cleverest person! His next statement, however, made me second guess my cleverness. He indeed knew me more than I did.

He gave me a steady look as he said, 'Do not become a slave of your own body.'

▼

Pihu underwent a blood transfusion as part of her ongoing treatment. She was better after a couple of days, but the last episode had made her extremely weak.

It was Sunday morning. I was busy doing nothing in my house, when someone knocked at the door. From the tone of the knock, I knew it was Annu. I scanned myself from top to bottom in the mirror. She had already knocked thrice by the time I ran a quick comb through my hair and opened the door.

She stood there in an elegant white salwar kameez. She always dressed simply, but smartly, complimenting herself. Simplicity does have its own beauty, I must say.

'Hi, Neel. How are you doing?'

'Quite well. Please come in!'

Truly speaking, I had started hating these formalities. I wished to address her and talk to her with more than those predefined questions - ...what are you doing... hope I have not disturbed you... and can we talk for a few minutes! They sound so silly.

'Any plan for Sunday?' she asked.

'Nothing as such... I am free.'

'Actually, Pihu is insisting on watching *Kung Fu Panda 3*. Why don't you come along if you have no specific plans for the day?'

I sensed loneliness in her voice. It underlined the absence of relatives or friends in her life. A common trend in metropolitan cities. People live in big houses, but there are no relatives and friends to visit.

'*Kung Fu Panda*? Err... isn't that a Chinese movie?' I asked, shuffling my hair with my right hand, trying to look decent while I asked a dumb question.

'It's not a Chinese movie. Actually... it's an animation movie. The protagonist Panda dreams of becoming a great warrior. It's quite popular among kids... and grown-ups....'

There was an enthusiasm in Annu's explanation. I had a feeling she too liked that character, rather than just Pihu. I had heard about this Panda, but had certainly not been interested.

'There is no obligation… you feel free to say no….' Annu said as an afterthought.

This is dangerous. When someone says there is no obligation.

I smiled, 'I would love to come along.' I tried to make sure my excitement did not seem as fake as it was.

'Thank you, this will make Pihu very happy.'

We booked tickets for the matinee show. Annu drove us to the E Square mall, near Shivaji station, in her red Maruti K10. Pihu was delighted. Throughout the ride, she leaned against the car door to support herself and keep upright. I thought of offering her support, but held back lest the silly girl took it as a hint.

168

E Square mall was flooded with humans. Well, it was a Sunday! We reached the theatre and found our seats. I had been into a movie hall after a very long time. Pihu happily took the middle seat.

Being in movie halls was nostalgic to me. I remember, when I went to see *Cleopatra, The Beautiful Vampire*. The movie was all about a few nude ladies, dressed like a vampire, undressing themselves so that the vampire could come and suck their blood. My childhood was spent in watching such rubbish, in the name of movie.

'Stand up, Neel. The national anthem is about to begin.' Annu poked me, bringing me back to reality. Pihu also stood up for the anthem, leaning on my shoulder for support. I did not offer any resistance. It was only for fifty-three seconds, after all, and I appreciated her spirit for the anthem.

We wore our 3D glasses, and the movie began with a fat panda, who was probably the dragon warrior... He was fighting against someone to save the valley. I heard the cheers and laughter in the hall. The panda's moves and facial expressions were funny, but they did not appeal to me. I lost my interest after twenty minutes or so. I was getting bored. An entire movie around a panda was too much to handle!

But Pihu was smiling. She looked so happy. I looked at Annu. She was watching silently, without any expression. I looked around me, at the audience; most of them were families.

I dragged my attention back to the movie. The character of the warrior panda was humorous. His antics made the audience laugh. At one point, we all laughed and Pihu caught hold of my palm. She behaved like an unwanted girlfriend. I wanted to shake her hand off, but Annu was there. Pihu was smiling, enjoying the show.

I realized that it was good to be a fool sometimes. It is not always right to go by reason. I allowed my hand to stay in hers.

Thirty

Annu was spending less time at work. I was helping her like an extended family member. Unsaid responsibilities had been given to me. Many unsaid promises were made. The best thing about unsaid promises is, there are no burdens, yet you are connected.

I readied my scrambled omelette with bread, and made myself a cup of tea. I was sitting on the plastic chair, considering taking up the interview offer from the school in Goa. I was on the verge of making a new relationship. A broken mother and a dying daughter – between both of them, there was hope. I decided, I should look for a job in Pune only.

I had almost finished my tea when there was a firm knock on the door.

'Why are you here, Pihu?'

She did not reply. She was panting, trying to catch her breath.

'Come inside… is everything fine? Why did you stress yourself so much to come here?'

'I need a favour, sir.'

I helped her to sit. 'What can I do for you?'

'I need to purchase something. Will you help me?'

'You want to go shopping?'

She nodded.

'Are you out of your mind?' I tried to be as polite as I could.

'No, it's very important stuff,' she said in all seriousness.

'I will get it for you. Tell me!'

'No, I have to purchase it myself. Please, it will just take fifteen minutes.'

Apart from Pihu's bad health, I had another major problem about this idea - money. What if she expected me to pay? How could I get rid of those unwanted shopping bills?

'I can help you only on one condition. If Annu is aware.' I looked at her sceptically.

'I already have mom's permission. You can call her and confirm, if you want.'

She was not smart enough to tell a lie. I said, 'That's not needed. But I do not have any cash, and my ATM card is not working.'

'I have the money!'

I loved that line! I wish I could say the same words on a daily basis. I had my bike, but I did not want to take any risk with Pihu. I booked a cab, and it came in ten minutes.

We climbed in and the driver turned the car around.

'Is this shopping so important? Even in this condition you are pushing yourself so hard.'

'Yes, tomorrow is an important day!'

'What is it?'

'Let's wait, sir.'

We reached Archie's Gallery in seven minutes.

'You want to come?' she asked me, walking into the gift store.

'No. You carry on, I will wait here.' I wasn't interested in whatever she was up to.

She nodded and went inside. I breathed a sigh of relief. I was far away from any expenditure. There was a Crossword book store next to the gift shop, and I strolled into it. I never found book shops too crowded, so I liked it in there. Every mall has its day, every shopping area has some or the other promotional events, but these Crosswords were always empty. I flipped through some of the books.

I came out soon after and about ten minutes later, I got a call. She had finished her shopping. It was weird. How could a girl finish shopping in ten minutes? Maybe she had something specific to buy.

We hired a ride to head back home.

'What did you buy?'

'A gift.'

I didn't ask who it was for.

'Can I ask you something?' she asked with her gaze fixed on me. It gives me chills whenever she asks my permission to *ask* a question. 'Do you like my mom?'

'Excuse me. What kind of a question is this?'

'I know you like my mom.'

My expression was like a squirrel caught with a solitary nut when on a hunger strike! I was speechless. How should I be reacting to her nonsense? But then, I was suddenly worried. Had this girl guessed what I was trying with her mother?

'Why are you asking then? Seems like you already know everything!'

'I just wanted to check your facial expression.'

I took a deep breath, contemplating killing her. I decided to change the topic.

'What did you shop for in just ten minutes?'

'A card.'

'For whom?'

It was hard to comprehend her facial expression. She smiled mischievously.

'It is for you.'

Thirty-one

Isat surrounded by my books. No, not the erotic novels that kept me hooked, but the mathematics textbooks. I was comparing the exercises in the various books. If faced with the question of which book helps kids learn better, I wanted to present a complete analysis of what was available in the market and which would be most effective. I was sure I could make the St Anthony School management give me the job. I was going to nail the interview! And then live here in Pune… happily ever after. Some days back I had found out that St Anthony School had a branch in Pune as well. This information had increased my interest in the interview tremendously, and I was really working hard for it.

My ground-breaking research was interrupted by the knock on the door followed by a voice, 'Neel…'

She called me with an authority, and I didn't like it, because I loved it.

I opened the door.

'Hi, Neel. What are you doing?'

'Nothing Annu… just preparing for an interview… in Goa.'

'Oh!' Her face changed visibly, '…will you be shifting to Goa then?'

I could read her discomfort. I smiled internally, wishing I could express my own feelings.

'Not really. They have a branch here in Pune too, but their recruiter sits in Goa.'

'Oh… great!' Her face turned jovial again.

'I need a small favour. I have to go to the hospital and Pihu is unwell. She is taking rest. I have arranged her lunch and everything… in case she requires any help, could you please keep an eye on her and keep me informed?' She looked at me confidently.

'Going to the hospital? Today is Sunday!'

'Yeah… some emergency operation has come up.'

'Okay! Don't worry about Pihu.'

She smiled. My cunning mind said this was the right time to hit the nail on the head. 'Wait, Annu. I have to give you something…'

She nodded. I came to my room and picked up a bundle of notes. Back at the door, I handed it to her, smiling softly with a fake self-respect expression. Internally, I prayed to a million unknown gods that she reject my fake generosity.

'What is this?'

'Rent for the past three months.' Believe me, no one could beat the confidence on my face.

'Don't be silly! You can do this later.' She said with authority.

She rejected my benevolence. I didn't insist a second time.

Before leaving, she turned around and said, 'Neel, you are not just our tenant.'

▼

When my door was knocked this time, I knew it was Pihu. I did not move an inch. She knocked again, urgently.

I realised she was unwell. I opened the door.

'How are you, Neel...' She was panting.

She had addressed me by my name. No "sir" ...nothing! It was a tough blow.

She was leaning against the wall, so I ignored everything and helped her inside, making her sit. 'Why have you come here... in this condition?'

She still was trying to catch her breath. 'Is everything fine? Shall I call your mother?'

'No. I'm fine, sir.'

I brought her a glass of water. 'Why have you come here? You could have called me upstairs. You should go back to your room and rest.'

'I will go in a minute. Just had to give you this.' She handed me a card.

Teachers receive plenty of cards of all sizes and ostentation, on various occasions. This one's size and texture said it was expensive. The glittery pastel envelope was covered with words like *trust, love, care, support* self-printed in a deeper hue.

I noticed that my fingers were shaking. Six months ago, I had received a card from Ananya. 'I cannot take this card...' I handed it back to her.

'You have to....' She dropped the card on the table and began walking heavily towards the door. I helped her to the first floor, instructing her not to come down again and calling me instead.

Well, I could not think of any occasion that merited a card. I picked it up from the table and threw it in the dustbin.

She knew very well that I liked her mom, she had said so herself on various occasions, and still she had dared to give me a card!

I finished my lunch and was all set to dive between the sheets for some fun and a late afternoon nap. I pulled the curtains close, switched off the light and increased the fan speed. Eyes closed, I was all set to enter my dream land. But then there was a tap – not on the door, but inside my head. I had a feeling this was the same card which she had purchased yesterday. I wondered what special occasion it was today. Why did she have to purchase that card even when she was so severely ill?

I left my bed and went to fetch the card from the bin. I switched on the light and opened the card.

Hi Neel sir,
Because of you, I believe in angels…
Happy Father's Day!

Thirty-two

I read the card over and over again. I looked up from the card to catch my image in the mirror. I saw a man who looked similar to Pihu's father. For the first time, I saw a person in the mirror who was not me.

The person in the mirror was answering all the questions that had troubled me for so many days now. Everything fell into place. Pihu had wanted me here because I looked like her father. The truth was far different from "the worst" I had assumed of Pihu. She disliked Ananya because she thought Ananya was talking nonsense about me. Realisation soon dawned as to why she had complained about Ananya. Why she had held my hand in the movie hall. All because she saw her father in me!

Pihu was not what I had so far thought her to be. Incidents since Pihu had offered her house on rent to me outside that broker's office began to play in front of my eyes. Every time she had barged into the house, all the times I had jeered at her, and she had responded just with an immature smile. Before long, my mind was too numb to think anymore.

And then out of nowhere a voice said, "…she is going to be dead soon…" A fear of life follows the fear of death.

A GIRL TO REMEMBER

The person in the mirror was still staring at me. I hated him. I hated how self-centred he was! There was something about the eyes that I was uncomfortable with. Since my hands remained immovable, frozen, I could not reach for the eyes and see. A couple more drops continued, wetting my cheeks, making way to my dry lips. I tasted the salty tears. The last time I remembered resorting to tears was when I was in class third.

It was one of those moments in life when your mind, heart, and eyes stop talking to each other. I was not shocked. I was not emotional. I was not happy, and all of a sudden, I was not me.

I remained confined in my house for the next twenty-four hours. I did not go to meet Pihu or Annu. I could not bring myself to face them.

Next day, summoning all the courage, I went to see Pihu. Annu opened the door and moved aside to welcome me inside the house.

'How is Pihu? Can I see her?'

This was not the first time I had made checking after Pihu's health my excuse, but today I was there only for Pihu.

'She is not doing well. Extremely weak… she has been in bed all morning.' Annu spoke like a concerned mother.

'Can I see her?'

'Of course.' She waved me towards Pihu's room, 'Would you like some tea?'

'Tea would be good,' I replied, though I didn't really feel the need for it. I agreed only so that I could have some time alone with Pihu.

My weak Pihu was lying on her bed. She was in pain. Her suffering was evident on her face. It was suddenly hard to accept.

A child was being punished like this for no mistake of hers. She was just an innocent girl. Her simplicity made her the cutest girl I had ever known. Here she was struggling in pain, yet she smiled as her eyes rested on me.

'How are you, sir?'

'Oh, I don't care about me... How are you?' I placed my shaking fingers on her head. I did not care to consider anymore, if I had the authority to do so.

'Why did you not come to see me yesterday?'

'I was busy... preparing for my job interview.'

'Did you like my gift?' she asked guilelessly.

'It was an awesome gift! The best till date, I will say.'

'Really? Then where is my return gift...?'

This girl was beyond my understanding. 'Tell me, what could I gift you, Pihu?'

'Will you give me what I ask for?'

'Well, I will try my best.'

She smiled. 'Will you marry my mom?'

Thirty-three

How could a girl of her age ask for things like that? She was so young... so innocent. How could I say yes? Or no, for that matter? Things were turning out just the same as I wanted them to. I had spent hours cooking plans to impress Annu. But when Pihu asked me to do it for her, it was not the same.

I felt I did not deserve to be Annu's husband. Realisation is a matter of becoming conscious of that, which is already real.

That night, again, I was not able to sleep, and was trying my best to not venture to the terrace. I was worried that Annu might be there. It was now almost a ritual to see each other on the terrace each night. I did not want to face her. I didn't know why, though. I might have been running from myself.

It was half past one and I was still wide awake. It was quite late and assumed Annu might have left the terrace by now.

I finished my second peg of whiskey and moved towards the terrace. Like all my assumptions in the past, this one was also wrong. She was there. Perhaps waiting for me.

'Annu... You are still here?'

She nodded, not saying a word. She had been crying. She had many reasons to.

'Why are you so late?' she sniffed, not looking at me.

'You look upset…'

She turned to face me. She looked lost in the moonlight. The tears refused to stop.

I am sure she needed a human touch. She needed to be comforted. She was expecting a hug, of course. But I did not give her that solace. Placing my hands on her shoulders, I said, 'Everything will be fine.'

This was the worst I could have come up with! But the acceptance that you could do nothing was all we had. You could only chant the same meaningless words in such situations – *Everything will be fine.*

'I don't know… Neel. What would be fine? How can it be?' She shook her head as if shaking off a thought, 'I don't care anymore. I have had enough of all this.'

I stood there like a rock. I didn't move a bit.

She waited for a few seconds, 'No one can help me…'

I intentionally kept back words of sympathy. I did not offer any false hopes… any commitments.

'How much time do we have?'

She understood what I was asking. 'I am not sure… a couple of weeks… one month… maximum.'

This rattled me harder than I had imagined. Till a few days back, I was running away from Pihu. Now I wished I could have some more time to live with her.

'Can I help you in any way, Annu?'

'Neel, I do need help from you.'

'Anything. Anything at all…'

'Pihu sees her father in you. She has this very silly thing in her head, that before she dies… she wants us to be… umm… settled.'

I had been wondering whether Annu was aware of Pihu's wish or not. This had clarified that doubt for sure.

'What do you want me to do?'

'Could you act like my... partner?'

Suddenly, it felt like the universe was supporting me. And here I was, a totally changed man.

'Neel, I am sorry I am dragging you into this. But can you do this for her? Is it possible? Please.' Annu poked me again.

The least I could do was support them. 'What do you need me to do, so that we look more than friends.'

'You just need to call me with my name... and spend some time with me in the kitchen. Rest, I will manage. Pihu should feel we are together.' She rattled off, like she had a plan ready. She had been giving it deep thought, and I, for once, wanted to be of help to someone.

Here was a mother, whose daughter was dying, putting everything on stake to fulfil her daughter's crazy wish. A dying girl wanting her mom to settle before she took her last breath. And the exact opposite to their selfless love, here I was, stuck in between a mom and a daughter.

If nothing else, I was sure of one thing – Pihu had planned everything very carefully and wanted to see everything in place before she left. Pihu was not an immature girl.

Thirty-four

Summer holidays were finally over. I was getting interview calls from various places. Earlier, I had turned down any opening outside Pune. Now I was open to an opportunity anywhere in India. I got an interview call from Christ College, Bangalore. If I could clear the first round of interviews anywhere, I would have to take a few trial classes. The hiring process would need 2-3 days to complete.

I went to see Pihu. She was in her bed, one leg out of the blanket. I saw a naked leg, and my gaze did not falter. I sat on Pihu's bed, close to her. I had no hesitation. There was no testosterone, no adrenalin rush, no hormonal imbalance.

A mind that is stretched by a new experience can never go back to its old dimensions.

'How are you, Pihu?' I asked lovingly.

She gave the same signature smile which she always had, but I had never understood. 'I am good. I have pain here.' She touched around her lower abdomen, '…and these medicines make me sleep all the time.'

'The pain will be over soon.'

'I know,' she replied.

We were not on the same page, I knew.

'So, when are you guys getting married?' she asked.

'Who said we are getting married?'

'No one. That is why I am asking you,' she said with a childlike smile.

The best way to avoid any question is to ask another. 'Why do you think I am suitable for your mom? Only because I resemble your father?'

'No. Not at all.' She gave her next words some thought.

It was rare to see her think before speaking. '…because you are my angel.'

▼

Dr Vedant visited every alternate day. Pihu's condition worsened with every passing day. They needed to visit the hospital quite often. I accompanied them twice. The situation was slipping out of hands, just as Pihu was slipping away from us. Annu knew exactly what to do. All insurances were in place, and most of the times, she administered treatment to Pihu at home. She was an expert in her duties, observing and recording patients' readings, coordinating with physicians and other healthcare professionals for creating and evaluating customized care plans.

Annu asked me to have dinner with them the next day. I wanted to say no, because it meant additional burden for a busy mother. But I agreed, for Pihu. Honestly. I went to her room, straight. Pihu was watching an animated movie. She had become thinner and her hair had curls. She was in her bed room all the time. She was on supplementary intravenous fluids, a small plastic tube put into her vein using a needle.

'Hey, I have some good news. I got a few interview calls,' I tried to sound cheerful.

'Wow! That is indeed great news. Which school?'

'One in Goa, and another in Bangalore.'

'That's bad news...' Her face lost whatever glow she was left with.

'Why? What is the problem?'

'Mom will need to change cities then.'

She was amazingly single-tracked and constantly weird, all the time. But I guess, I had accepted her the way she was. I smiled and replied, 'So what? Your mom will come along with me. It's not that bad an idea.'

'Your mom? Stop addressing her like that. Say, Annu will also go along with me.'

I groaned.

'Guys, sorry to interrupt you two. Dinner time.' Annu entered and saved me.

'Okay mom.' Her voice was euphoric.

With the kind of equation I shared with my family, I never knew what being important to someone felt like. It was hard to believe that Pihu was so happy because she was having dinner with me!

Her mom pulled out the bed-table for her. She usually took dinner on her bed because she was too weak to get up.

'Not today. I want to eat at the dining table.'

'You do not have enough strength,' Annu countered.

It was hard for Pihu to sit for more than fifteen minutes without support. But she wasn't the one to give up.

'Let me try this time, Annu,' I intentionally addressed her by her name. I had never done that in front of Pihu till now. It was always ma'am or Annu ji.

I helped Pihu to stand. It was easier for her to walk with a support. She sat on a chair that could support her sideways too. It was the first time we were sharing a meal.

Dinner is always better when we eat together. My mind instantly went back to recall, when was the last time I had had any family dinner.

'How is the food, Neel?' Annu asked

'Delicious.' I was being honest, and my heart filled with a strange joy as it was the first time that we were having a candid chat, without any formal sir or madam. And to top it, our little silly girl kept smiling throughout the meal.

'What is your favourite dish, Neel sir?' Pihu asked munching on her bite. The speed at which she was eating was a clear indicator she was not interested in food. 'I love Dum aloo and dal makhani.'

'I also like dal makhani,' I said with a smile and offered my palm up for a high-five, which she slowly clapped.

We dived into a discussion of food when the nurse mother ruled, 'No talking during dinner, guys.'

The head of the family had pronounced, and we went silent. I had almost finished my dinner while Pihu was still struggling with the chapati.

'What happened, Pihu? Any problem? Why are you so slow in eating today?'

'I have an important question to ask.'

Annu and I looked at each other. We realized a bomb was in store.

'When are you guys getting married?' Pihu asked as a mother would ask her kids, when they would settle, so that she could rest in peace.

'Stop talking, Pihu! It's dinner time,' Annu said.

'Very soon, Pihu,' I said, and of course, that brought a smile on her face.

She went back to her food with great satisfaction, but stopped eating after a few minutes. I thought she had had enough.

'Do you want to go to bed?' Annu enquired.

She shook her head. 'Can I ask a question to both of you?'

She always asked dangerous question and she didn't really care if she had the permission to do that or not.

'Tell me your best moment in life...' she looked at us with wide eyes.

'Stop behaving like a moron. It's time for bed,' Annu said sharply.

'Please...' Pihu said with a plastic face.

'When your mom accepted my love,' I lied. Annu was almost shocked, but she knew very well that those were the words which would make Pihu happy.

'For you?' she looked at her mother.

Her mom made a face. 'I am not going to answer your stupid questions.'

'Mom, please.'

Annu raised her eyebrows, but finally, she was the mom who had been attending to all her fancies for years.

'When you were born. That was the happiest day of my life.'

It looked like the moment of the last supper. Pihu stared at me. I took the cue and asked her the same question.

'Tell me you best moment, Pihu?'

'It's now. Having dinner as a family,' she said in a reflex action.

Something choked my insides. She had craved a family. The pain of an only child, without a father, was in front of me. Her next words made the dinner even more difficult for me.

'Can I call you Dad?'

'Enough of your nonsense, Pihu!' Annu screamed.

189

Thirty-five

I arranged all my certificates and experience letters, even that fat gold chain, and packed my luggage. I was all set to leave for Goa for the interview. I was feeling bad about leaving Annu alone. I needed this job. I had to do something in life.

In a far corner of my heart, I was getting claustrophobic. Both the mother and the daughter had constructed a larger than life image of mine. I did not have the courage to break the heart of the girl who was dying in a few days. I did not want to face her and tell a lie. I wanted to leave this house.

I had to text Annu that I was leaving for a week. My fingers rolled over the keypad and I wrote - *Take care of yourself and keep me posted about Pihu*. But then, I erased the message. My words would be fake. They could not change anything. I avoided meeting Pihu. I booked my radio cab and went out to wait for it. I looked at the house behind me. It was the place that had helped me when I was thrown out on to the streets and had nowhere to go. And then again, Pihu came to my mind. I felt, I was going to lose her.

On a whim, I cancelled the cab. I had to see Pihu.

Annu opened the door. She guessed I was ready to leave for the interview.

'Good luck, Neel!' she said.

She was transparent with her emotions. I could see, she was not happy. 'Thank you. May I see Pihu?'

She smiled and welcomed me in. Pihu was lying on her bed. She must have been restless, for she had kicked away her covers and I could see her bare and pale legs. Annu pulled on the covers to cover those naked legs, and it woke Pihu up.

'You want something, tea or coffee?'

'Tea,' I answered though I did not want anything.

'Where are you going?' Pihu saw my bag and guessed the rest.

'Goa! For the interview I told you about,' I answered cheerily. 'How are you, dear?'

'All the best, sir,' she said with a smile. It was not her signature smile.

'How are you?' I asked again.

'Very bad! Restless.' Then she looked at me and made a puppy face to say, 'Why are you going for the interview?'

'Because it has to be done. And you are not allowed to speak much.'

'I know. What will you bring for me from there?'

'What do you want?' I asked eagerly, looking forward to promise her whatever I could.

She thought for a few seconds. I wondered what this little crazy girl would come up with this time.

'I want you to come back with a good story.'

'Why do you want a story?'

'I am fed up with mom's stories. I want new stories from my father.'

Whenever she addressed me as her father, it pinched a part of my heart.

'I will come back with the best love story for you.'

I could see that the medicines were making her drowsy. She was trying hard to stay awake. So I made her lie back, kissed her on her forehead and said, 'I will come back soon. Please wait for me.'

She understood and nodded.

Sometimes it is difficult to control your emotions. I don't know why I was flooded with them. This was the reason I had not wanted to meet her before leaving. I did not know how to handle them.

I went close to her and whispered in her ears, 'You can call me Dad.'

Thirty-six

The interview and demo classes were scheduled on different days. All demo classes and preliminary interviews went well. As the principal was not available, I was asked to stay back for another day, for one to one discussion with the principal.

I was free in the evening, so I called up Annu. She told me that Pihu was not doing well. Then suddenly she disconnected the call. I assumed she had broken into tears and did not want me to hear them. I should have been there. But I was neither a doctor nor an angel. Pihu had everything and everyone who could help her.

I was getting bored and thought of visiting one of the beaches. I hired an auto and went to the Calangute beach. While I sat alone at the shore, I saw people enjoying their evening. Kids were busy making sand houses, youngsters were frolicking in the water, playing with the waves. Few were drinking beer in the shacks while girls were busy pouting and taking selfies. I was the only one sitting and watching all of them, alone.

The beach was full of girls wearing short skirts, bathing suits, bikinis, and half pants. I did notice the abundance of naked legs.

I had spent my life looking out for them. Chasing a glimpse. But now, I did not feel anything for them. I smoked a few joints, but nothing excited me as it once had.

The sun was at the horizon, painting the clouds saffron. It was a sight people dream of. I noticed a young couple with a kid. The child was busy playing with sand and the parents were helping him out with interest. I watched them for a long time. There was happiness on the beach, which I was not a part of. My cigarette joint had burnt to ashes, and so had my spirit, it seemed. Then a voice halted my thoughts.

'Sir, can you please take a picture of us?' The man of the family called out.

I left my spot and captured their happiness in two pictures. That guy came to me, collected the camera, and checked the photos. I still remember his words, 'It's a perfect family picture. Thank you!'

I am not sure why that line touched me so much.

The next day, I had a fruitful interaction with the school principal. I was all set to start for Pune. I decided on catching the evening bus from Mapusa.

I called Annu, twice. But she did not take my calls, nor did she call back. I was scared. Yet I was sure if something *drastic* had happened, Annu would surely have called. My mind kept going back to Pihu. I was missing her.

The journey by bus was troublesome. I was never comfortable travelling by bus; I prefer trains. Around 4 a.m., I heard the bus conductor shouting, 'Satara... the passengers who want to get down at Satara... get down here. The bus will be in Pune in two hours...'

Why was this guy shouting at the top of his voice, I thought in my sleep-fuzzled state.

'Hey, bhaiya! This bus will be going to Pune only... Why are you shouting?'

'This bus is terminating at Mumbai, sir. Be ready for Pune in two hours. Else you will land in Mumbai.' He smiled, showing his tobacco stained teeth.

I nodded at his unpleasant tone.

His mention of Mumbai made me recall suddenly, mom would be there. I clearly remembered the dates she had mentioned. Last week she would have come to Mumbai, and would be staying there for a month. It was not like, I was missing her. The name of the city had rung a bell. I realized my brother Nikhil and sister-in-law Neha would be there. Yes, my entire family was there.

Soon enough, the conductor started howling, 'Pune! Pune!'

I was puzzled. This was my destination.

'Pune... those who want to get down, please come forward.' The conductor screamed.

I didn't get down. Maybe I had made up my mind or the confusion to not get down at Pune prevailed.

We crossed Lonavala. Nikhil's home was only one hour from there. My mind argued, *why are you going to his house? You never cared for family earlier?* But there was no explanation.

I got down at the Vashi bus stop and hired an auto. The best thing in Mumbai is you need not negotiate with the autowallahs. They will follow the metre, fair and square. Everyone knows Hindi. Sometimes it was difficult to believe you were in Maharashtra. I asked the autowallah, 'Sanpada, Mumbai?'

'Where in Sanpada?'

'Near Gurudwara. Millennium Society…'

After twenty minutes or so, I stood outside the society. I was all set to make my move when the society's guard stopped me.

'Visitor?'

'Yes, a visitor.'

'Whom do you want to meet, sir?'

'Nikhil Kumar…'

He extended the visitor's register for me to enter my name. He helpfully told me the direction, 'Fourth floor, second flat. But sir is not at home.'

'When did he go out?'

'A few minutes ago, with madam.'

That must be Neha, I thought. The confusion in my mind, to go or not to go, ended. I could go and meet mom, and maybe leave before the two of them got back. I was waiting outside the lift when my phone rang.

'How are you, Annu? Why did you not answer my calls?' I fired questions as soon as I took the call.

'Neel, where are you?' was all that she said. There was a sincere worry in her voice. She was missing me.

'I am on my way to Pune. What happened? Is everything … well?'

She did not say anything.

'I will be back soon, Annu. Stay strong. Just a couple of hours, I promise!'

'Pihu is critical, Neel!'

For a moment, I thought I should abandon my plans to meet mom. But I was only a few steps away. And there was something

I wanted to say to her. I gathered courage and moved towards the flat. Each step I took got heavier as it got burdened with emotions. I was recollecting my entire life with those footsteps. I was wondering if I would ever be able to face Neha again. Or my brother Nikhil. I thanked my luck that they were not there.

I stood outside the flat, reading the nameplate - Neha & Nikhil Kumar.

I read my brother's name with Neha. I realized all over again how much I had hurt him. How difficult it would be for my brother, who knew everything about Neha and me. I was jealous that he was so strong as to forgive her.

I knocked at the door. With every passing second, my heartbeat ran a marathon. I expected my mother to open the door any second, and I would hug her.

I was dumbfounded. I did not know what to say or where to look. She had not been expecting me, either.

'Hi Neha!' I finally said.

She was blank. She did not even reply to my formal 'hi'. The lady who had gone out with Nikhil had been mom.

'How are you?' Her dazed face and nervous voice said my presence was unwanted.

'I am good.' My lost face would have said otherwise.

'You are here to meet your brother?'

To tell you the truth, I was not sure who I was there for. I nodded in response.

'No one is home. And I am sorry, I cannot invite you inside the house, especially in the absence of the other family members.'

How life had changed! She was the same woman who had once been involved with me, open to my touch and caresses. We

197

always prayed for moments when no one would be home. And today, I was struggling to even talk to her.

'I can understand.'

'Are you okay?

'Yes.'

She hesitated and asked, 'Do you want money?'

I never called them on any festival. Never wished them on their birthdays... What else could she have thought?

'No, I don't want any money.' I looked around. 'I will leave. Maybe... come some other time.'

I picked my bag, was about to turn and leave when she called out, almost in panic, 'Neel...! I have a request to make...'

'Yes please.'

'Please do not come here. It will be very difficult for Nikhil to see you.'

I looked at my own feet, nodding in understanding her request. 'Can I ask you something?'

She nodded.

'How did Nikhil get to know about us?'

'I confessed... about... er... what happened between us... one day.'

'And you did not think it was necessary to take me into confidence?' I looked up at her.

'It was my confession, not yours. When I was cheating on Nikhil with you, I found it difficult to sleep. It started hurting me every day. I wanted peace. I decided I could not ride on two boats, so I confessed everything to my husband,' she said agitated, but confidently.

'How did Nikhil react? He did not punish you?'

'Confession is the greatest punishment, Neel. And Nikhil is a great human being.' She had said many things in those words.

I could do nothing but nod, and then asked her, 'Why did you think I have come here for money?'

'Nikhil said you are going through a rough patch in life and may try to contact me for money. He even said I could give you some cash.'

I had used my family only for money. I remained silent. She drew a different conclusion from my silence.

'Do you want some cash? Tell me how much? After all, we are family.'

'No.' For the first time in my life, I understood the meaning of family. A brother, who could not bear to see me, was trying to help me even though he hated me so much. I had no courage to stand there. I turned and pressed the lift's call button.

Neha drew the door to close it shut. I called out, 'Wait a second, Neha!'

I unzipped the bag I was carrying, and from an inner pocket, I pulled an object out and said, 'I came here to return this.'

I opened my palms and gave that stolen gold chain. 'I did not come here for money. I have come here for my family.'

Thirty-seven

Suddenly the urgency to meet Pihu increased multiple times. Till a few days back, all I wanted was to avoid her. It was not mood swing. It was something beyond, which I can't explain to you. I reached Pune in three hours, anxious to the core, almost running on my toes.

Leaving my luggage at the door, I climbed the steps to the first floor. I was about to knock on the door when I noticed the lock. The dirt around the floor mat said, no one had been home for a few days.

My phone rang. I picked the call before it could ring properly. 'Hi, Annu...'

'Neel, have you arrived?' Annu's voice was all panic.

'Yes, Annu, where...'

'We are at Aditya Birla hospital. Come fast, Neel!'

She shared the ward details. I unlocked my flat, dumped my bag, and kick-started my bike in record time. I was on my way to the hospital, and my mind was burdening me with memories all through the way.

I suddenly repented going for those interviews. I could have waited for a few more days.

I reached Aditya Birla hospital. Annu was standing outside the private room, talking to someone. I had a million questions and an urgency to see her. I did not wait for Annu to finish her conversation with whoever it was.

'Pihu?' I looked at Annu and asked.

Annu did not reply. When the other person left, she came to me and hugged me. Then she gave in to her tears. The good thing about hugs is, when you give one, you get one too. Had life not given me reasons to suffer, I would never have known the healing power of a hug.

Was everything… over? I could not bring myself to ask.

'How is Pihu, Annu?' I held her shoulders and pushed her back to an arm's length to know the answer.

'Last stage.' She said amidst sobs, 'She has been waiting for you, I guess.'

I was distraught and couldn't utter a word. 'Internal bleeding started on the day you left for Goa. We arranged a few blood donors… but this time, her body did not respond. She is extremely weak… was barely able to breathe. We shifted her to the hospital. We have been here for the last two days…Since I am a nurse, we were able to avoid shifting her to the ICU,' Annu recounted what she had been dealing with.

I walked in. My Pihu slept peacefully. She was dressed in a green hospital gown. There was a deep silence, barring the few beeps and buzzes from the devices attached to her. Her eyes were shut, and the pale face was largely covered with an oxygen mask. I was content to see her sleep and did not want to wake her up. The white sheets covering her could not hide the tubes coming out from her body. She was bound by them, practically not in a condition to move. The six screens around her showed some numbers I couldn't make head or tail of.

I sagged into the chair next to the bed. I touched her forehead, but she did not move. Pihu had been given some high doses of medicine, I was told, sending her into long phases of deep sleep. Her current unconsciousness was one such. I waited for her to gain consciousness. I was not even sure if she would wake up. Even once. But Annu had said maybe she was waiting for me. I hoped she would.

My wait was unending, and minutes swiftly changed to hours. I was recollecting the days spent with her. How she had argued with me for small things. How she never cared what I was doing and walked in whenever she felt like. How endlessly she insisted to play Ludo with me. Some of those memories made me smile, and all of them made me miss her terribly.

I got restless. I left the chair and started strolling in the room. Annu understood there was something on my mind. After two hours of waiting, Pihu finally opened her eyes. I was excited and happy to see her conscious; she had opened her eyes to see me.

As soon as Pihu opened her eyes, she whispered, 'Hi... Pihu, I am back. The interview was good. I got the job as well.'

She smiled. I wanted to capture that smile. I held her hand gently, but Annu's face crumpled on seeing this deeply emotional rendezvous.

'Now you go to sleep. Don't worry about anything. I will not leave your side, I promise.'

She moved her head slightly.

202

I stood there for a few minutes. Pihu fidgeted again. I guessed she wanted to say something. Annu came beside her and removed the mask covering her mouth.

She whispered, 'What have you brought for me... from Goa?'

Annu put the mask back.

I looked at her face. 'I told you... I would come with a story.'

Her lips moved fractionally, resembling a smile.

I thought about the story. This would probably be the last story for her. I looked at Annu. I saw a loving mother holding her daughter who was heading towards a one-sided lane of life.

My eyes fell on the room's mirror. Here was a mother who was ready to do anything for her daughter's life and then there was cute little Pihu. All she wanted was to see her mom with a companion before she left. And then there was a Neel, whom I knew since ages. There were invisible tears in his eyes. I thought, what could I possibly tell her. In that moment, Neha's words came back to me like a sudden revelation – *confession is the best punishment*. I had to punish myself before it got too late.

I sat on her bed and asked, 'You wanted to hear the story of an angel and a demon?'

She smiled.

'I am a bad storyteller, Pihu, but I promise I will try my best. I would even write a story someday and let people know about the demon and the angel. That will help the world remember the real angel, you see!'

There was a little spark in Pihu's eyes. Annu looked curious about the story as well.

'There lives an angel and there is a demon,' I started off after a deep breath. Both sets of eyes were glued to my face, trying to anticipate the story.

I help Pihu's hand, but it lay in mine, limp.

'The angel's name is Pihu, and the demon ... Neel.

'One day, the demon Neel was thrown out of the school he taught in, because of his dishonourable activities... He had nowhere to go. And that's when angel Pihu offered him her home to stay in. She thought, this guy looks just like my father. God has sent my father back... in a different form.

'Pihu believed in angels, because her mother had told her a demon had taken her father away and an angel was going to set everything right again. Pihu thought... Neel was the one. She started caring for him and supported him in every possible way. But the demon, Neel, did not wish to have anything to do with Pihu and Annu. He was a practical man, who did not care for anything other than his own interests. He displayed fake concern and love for both the ladies, and in return enjoyed living in their house for free. Not to mention, he got a family that loved him dearly, without his having to do anything.

'Neel's only purpose in life was... to fulfil his body's cravings, and to earn a lot of money. He was a slave of his needs and desires. He never respected women, ever since he was a child perhaps. He treated them like a soft toy. He was so bad, he even didn't spare his teachers when he was in school...'

Suddenly I couldn't go on anymore. Annu was stunned into silence with my narration and was covering her mouth with her hand. Pihu's face was difficult to read, but she looked at me unblinkingly. I had to finish what I had started, so I went on nonetheless.

'Then the demon got to know... that Annu was the owner of the property. He made it his aim to win Annu's heart... so that someday, he could marry her and become the indirect owner of the expensive property in the posh locality. That way, he wouldn't have to do anything and he would still be rich. He started sympathising with Annu and helped her in all possible ways. He took advantage of innocent Pihu... to win Annu's heart.

'Then one day, in a weak moment, Annu told Neel that Pihu only had limited time to live. Neel was unaffected. Why would he care for someone who he had nothing to do with! And even that did not make him feel bad. Rather, he treated that as an opportunity to become a shoulder for Annu to cry on. All this was a part of the demon Neel's plan, but the angel Pihu still believed in him, blindly.

'But let me confess, my daughter, my Pihu, that demon Neel didn't love your mom. He never loved her and neither did he love you.'

I gathered all the courage I had and looked at Pihu. It was the complex human state of being, sad and shocked at the same time. I looked at the mirror. Now I could face the man. I had no guilt now. Avoiding looking at Annu, I summoned my inner emotions and continued, 'But today, I am a different man, Pihu.'

She didn't utter a word, nor did she move a muscle. 'I do not deserve your mom, Pihu. She is the best mother god could carve. She has been strong for you, even when she was broken from inside. And no matter how you judge me after this revelation, I promise I will not leave her alone. I am not an angel you thought me to be, Pihu. You are the true angel, my daughter, who touched my life to make me a better person. We all have an angel and a demon inside us, and today, you have killed the demon inside me forever. If there is any living angel… that is you.'

I was losing hope of redemption when I finally got the signal I was dying for. Her limp hand was finally clutching mine.

I finished, delicately hugging my daughter to my heart, crying my soul out to her. I cried after many years and washed off all my guilt with it. I didn't care about the world; I only cared about Pihu when I said, 'Please forgive me, my daughter. Please forgive your demon…'

Epilogue

My angel passed on the same night. I thanked god that it happened when she was in deep sleep. She went on, and took the demon along.

Annu was broken, to say the least. But she is a confident woman, I know. She will pick the pieces of her life and start afresh.

Almost a month after not speaking to each other much and Annu trying to deal with her loss, she and I had a long discussion about the series of events and I made many confession. Again. And with every tear I shed, every mistake I confessed at having committed, I found a stronger angel inside me. My Pihu inside my heart.

Annu was aghast, but simply said, 'A true confession is the biggest punishment.'

We became friends again, and I could not expect much from her after what she had come to know about me. As I had promised my Pihu of telling the story to people, I started working on my book. This book, which has been written in the memory of my darling daughter. I asked mom, Aarav and Annu to contribute to the book by giving their perspective to the story too, and they obliged by sharing their honest thoughts. I tried to get Nikhil to say something too, but he denied. I knew it would be difficult for him to recollect all that again, and did not pester more than that.

I joined an international school near Pune, while Annu continues with her job of serving humanity.

In the time that has passed, I have come closer to my mother, and knowing of my change of heart, Nikhil had also warmed up to me a bit. He told me he wanted to give me a fair chance, and I would not let this chance go. He has been there for me whenever I needed him; now it was my turn to prove worthy of his affection.

It was one year that Pihu left us. Instead of mourning over her demise, Annu wanted to have a small puja and hold a gathering of people Pihu loved, so that her daughter's soul could rejoice in seeing her mother 'settled'. So, I helped her organise a small gathering in the same house, on the terrace. I sought permission to call my family and was granted. I wanted to introduce Annu to my family, because I had promised Pihu I wasn't going to leave her mother alone. No matter what! My mom was slightly reluctant, seeing her most handsome boy around a lady who was once married and was eleven years older. But she is a mother, and she knew nobody could have brought out the good man in me, if not her.

The surprise visitor was my father. I had not expected him and Nikhil to turn up, but they did, and I couldn't thank them enough. Annu had called over a few colleagues too, including Dr Vedant and everyone was trying to keep the mood cheerful, not allowing Annu's mood to dip even a bit. We all had dinner and missed Pihu terribly.

I looked up at the sky, found the brightest star and believed it to be Pihu watching over. I apologised to everyone, except Aarav. He and I are way beyond such formalities, and he knew.

That night, under the wide blue sky sparkling with stars, everyone found some lost relationship. Nikhil, Neha, my parents. And my best friend Aarav. Someone found his son, and someone found the lost brother, while someone found the best friend and Annu got back someone who she could rely on, as much as she could fall back on Mangesh. And I, after a very long time, saw a family. My family.

I went to the same corner where Annu spent hours seeing the Mula river. I missed my cute little daughter. She was no ordinary girl, but a girl for some higher purpose. She was born to teach me an important lesson – A woman is far more than just a body.